NEWS
from the
RANCH

Mia Francis

ISBN 978-1-68517-553-5 (paperback)
ISBN 978-1-68517-554-2 (digital)

Christian Faith Publishing
832 Park Avenue
Meadville, PA 16335
www.christianfaithpublishing.com

Illustrations by: Laura Beth Ramsay

All the small horse drawings are from "The Otto Girls"

Printed in the United States of America

The setting and main characters

These stories take place on a small ranch, actually, by Texas standards, a ranchette, somewhere in Central Texas. It is a "little bit of heaven on earth." And, sometimes, it is referred to as "Rancho Relaxo."

Primary areas

The Coastal Pasture: a pasture directly in front of the house
The Backyard Feed Line: in the backyard between two trees with birdfeeders in them
The Big Muddy: a big pond behind the house
The Feed Shed: a small shed near the house and also near the Well House
The Horse Shed: a shed in the small horse pasture behind the house
The Memorial Garden: a garden with plants for lost loved ones overlooking the Big Muddy
Poor Man's Pasture: a pasture north of the house sloping down the creek
The Big Sandy Pasture: a big pasture area near the front of the property
The Tugly Woods: a wooded area near the front of the property
Green Lips Pond: (aka Reflecting Pond, Pond of Despair) a pond near the Big Sandy Pasture
Frog Pond: a small pond near the front of the property
The Well House: (aka Toad Hall) a small shed with the well pump and equipment in it, near the house
The Dry Creek: a fork off of the creek that is dry most of the year
The Creek: (aka Sandy Creek, Pee Creek) a creek that runs through the property, dividing the property in half
The Various Riding Trails: these trails go through the different areas of the ranch and woods. Their names are Racehorse Lane, Cardinal Lane, Bones Trail, Junkyard Lane, Miniature Pony Lane, Primo Trail, Bird Trail, and Telephone Pole Trail

The main characters

The cats: Peekaboo and Phoenix. Peekaboo is male and is orange-and-white. Phoenix is female and is gray.
The horses: Prince, Carry, and Wiggles. Prince is a gelding. Carry is female and is Wiggles's mom. Wiggles is female.
The cows: Various cows that come and go. The cowboy tends to the cows.
The chickens: A few chickens lived for a short time at the ranch.
The ducks: Black-bellied whistling ducks show up at the ranch, as do other varieties of ducks.
The wild turkeys: A flock of wild turkeys inhabits the ranch.
The bobcat: Twiggy is the local bobcat occasionally seen at the ranch.
The wild hogs: Texas is blessed and cursed with wild hogs.
The caracara: (aka Mexican eagle) Phidippides and Penelope are the two-resident caracaras.
The deer: Various deer inhabit the ranch.
The rabbits, roadrunners, armadillos, skunks, coyotes, owls, and the like are all residents of the ranch.

Life on the Ranch Continues

Howdy, all:

Peekaboo, the orange-and-white cat, hopped onto the window ledge inside the house. He laid back his ears and snarled at the rooster, "Big Red." And, what was Big Red's response? He pecked at the window at Peekaboo! With that, Peekaboo fled under the table and sat there, staring back at the rooster.

Later that morning, Phoenix, the other cat, was sitting under the red chair looking at the piano. She had never done this. Wonder what was under the piano.

The piano was moved. Sure enough, there was a little field mouse. Peekaboo came to the rescue. He chased that mouse clear out to the garage and the great outdoors. Phoenix ran in the opposite direction and hid under the chair.

So one cat is afraid of the rooster while the other cat is afraid of a mouse. Hmmm. A bit topsy-turvy, wouldn't you say?

Life continues at the ranch in all its varieties. Here's hoping your life has some topsy-turvy!

TTFN,
Mia

The Cow Jumped over the Moon

Howdy, all:

Yesterday, the Lonely Bull was down by the fence near the Big Muddy, the pond behind the house. He was visiting some of the neighbor's cows.

Well, just as the nursery rhyme goes, "Hey, diddle, diddle, the cat in the fiddle, the cow jumped over the moon," the bull jumped over the five-foot fence as gracefully as any ballet dancer. There he was, visiting with the neighbor's cows and happy as he could be.

The bull's owner, the Cowboy, had to come later and get the Lonely Bull back from the neighbor's pasture. And, no, the bull didn't jump back over. He was led through the gap gate. Now he is back with *his* cows.

Things occasionally *jump* here at the ranch. Here's hoping things jump in your world.

TTFN,
Mia

Off to Horse School

Howdy, all:

Well, Wiggles, the young filly, went off to horse school this morning. She loaded right up into the trailer. But Prince, the gelding, and Carry, her momma, were so excited about her being the trailer that they ran alongside across the bridge and probably were going to run clear to horse school with Wiggles!

So, they were put into a smaller pasture while Wiggles was driven off. The cacophony of whinnies and neighing was quite something.

Wiggles got off the trailer at the school and went right into the round pen. She has already made *friends* and has had her first session. She did quite well. Early next week, she will have the saddle and bridle put on. That should be interesting.

Life on the ranch is always an education. Here's to your education. May it never end.

TTFN,
Mia

Cow Poetry
Damn the Electric Fence! Damn the Electric Fence!

Howdy, all:

Perhaps some of you remember the *Far Side* comic of "Cow Poetry...damn the electric fence! Damn the electric fence!" Here on the ranch, there was an adventure with the cows and the electric fence.

The other morning, the Lonely Bull was lying on the back patio, just sunning himself next to the lawn chairs as if he were king. Dolly Madison, one of the cows, and her merry band of calves had led the charge through the electric fence into the yard. Because as everyone knows, the grass is really greener on the other side.

One can imagine it is a bit unsettling to find a bull at one's backdoor, especially before the caffeine has kicked in. The electric fence around the yard was repaired without delay, and the cows and the Lonely Bull were redirected back into the pasture.

So no more bull at the backdoor. And, here's hoping you have no bull either in your world.

TTFN,
Mia

4

Bull Fight

Howdy, all:

A peaceful morning was ended with loud thuds and crashes. An intruding bull, Sir Blanco, had invaded, and the Lonely Bull was fending off his territory.

It is quite a sight to see these massive creatures pushing and shoving each other. Their muscles ripple as they clash.

Now, how does one stop this? A shot in the air, will that stop it? It did not. They had pushed each other through the neighbor's fence and into the mesquite jungle. The crashing noises continued. The Lonely Bull's cowboy owner was summoned, and somehow, someway, the cowboy way, the bulls were separated. The fence was repaired. Peace was restored to the day.

Thus, the day once again was peaceful at the ranch. Sure hope your day can be filled with peace.

TTFN,
Mia

The Lonely Bull Lives up to His Name

Howdy, all:

The Telstar song, "The Lonely Bull," needs to be played for the Lonely Bull here at the ranch. He is his own character.

The other day, the entire cow herd and the three horses, Prince, Carry, and the filly Wiggles were all napping by the Big Muddy. But it was not the entire herd, for the Lonely Bull was missing. Now, where the heck could that big guy be? Had he jumped the fence again or had another fight with an intruder?

Finally, he was spotted, all by himself, under a tree at the far end of the pasture, having his very own bull nap!

The crew is all together here at the ranch. Sure hope your crew is together.

TTFN,
Mia

After the Big Rain

Howdy, all:

Last week, we had another heavy rain. The dry creek filled up with water and logs to the point of breaking the gap fence that spanned it. It is going to be quite a chore to clear the debris and fix that gap fence, but right now, there still is water running in the dry creek.

The roadrunners are out and about. There appear to be two making a home near Reflecting Pond. Reflecting Pond is the second pond on the ranch. It is tucked into the woods just off the Big Sandy Pasture.

Wiggles is continuing her training. She will get a saddle and a rider next week. It may be a good thing if the saddle has a seatbelt! She is a lively young horse and about to turn three next week. (She was born on April 18.)

The wildflowers of Central Texas are in full bloom after the rains. They make the pastures so very colorful.

So after the big rain, life at the ranch proceeds. Hope your life also proceeds.

TTFN,
Mia

Celebrating Mother's Day at the Ranch

Howdy, all:

Happy Mother's Day to all living and deceased.

Big Red, the rooster, continues with his daily morning wake-up calls. He and the remaining chickens continue to provide fresh eggs. The chicken population is dwindling due to invaders from the wild. Hard to pin down which critter is the culprit.

The wild turkeys have taken to hiding out deep in the mesquite woods. They are infrequently seen. In their place, two black-bellied whistling ducks have shown up. These ducks have found the birdfeeder and subsequent bird seed scattered in the backyard.

The cows, led by the Lonely Bull, had a celebratory dance for Mother's Day. All the cows, Crazy Cow, Dolly Madison, Clara, Willie, Ninety-Nine (her ear tag is number ninety-nine), and the others kicked up their heels and cavorted about as if they had just won the cow lottery. Green grass forever was the theme!

The motto on the ranch is "celebrate." May your world have a similar motto.

TTFN,
Mia

"Hotter than Heck"

Howdy, all:

Well, it is hotter than heck here in Texas. The temperature is at 103 today; yesterday, it was 109. And all the critters are seeking shade wherever they can find it.

There are two toads living in the Well House, now known as Toad Hall. The cool concrete floor and moisture are so very welcome to them.

Peter Cottontail, the rabbit living by the feed shed, really appreciates the bowl of water put out for him each day.

The horses are hiding in the glen by Reflecting Pond, also known as "Pond of Despair" (from *The Pilgrim's Progress*). The pond is shrinking from the evaporation due to the heat, thus the new name. But the horses do find that they can stay cool by keeping close by and soaking their feet in the mud. The cows also are staying near this pond.

All are doing their best to stay cool here at the ranch. May you also be cool.

TTFN,
Mia

The Training Continues

Howdy, all:

Wiggles has accepted the saddle. Now comes the part of training that teaches her that she is not the boss. She needs to learn the commands from both the cues of the bridle and subtle weight shifts. So figure eights and circles become part of her day.

Her penchant is to run and run fast. She really should have been born a race horse rather than a plucky little cow horse. Give her the open pasture, and off she goes galloping with abandon.

Prince, the elder gelding, watches her as she progresses through her training. He appears to be proud to have shown her a few things, such as how to cross a running creek without fear. (Her momma, Carry, is at another ranch so that Wiggles can be completely weaned.)

Life at the ranch continues to be a learning session. May your life continue to afford learning opportunities.

TTFN,
Mia

At the Back Door, at the Front Door

Howdy, all:

If anyone tells you that life in the country is quiet and serene, filled with peaceful scenes, tell them they do not know what they speak.

For example, this morning, at the backdoor, a squeak came, and both cats were staring at the back patio. A hummingbird was caught by its leg on the rug at the backdoor. He was freed and rested on the sage plant after his ordeal.

Then, later in the morning, a skunk showed up at the front door, and let the door have it! Unfortunately, Peekaboo, the orange-and-white cat, was in the range of the skunk's shot. Perhaps he was the offending creature that angered the skunk. Poor Peekaboo had to suffer a tomato juice bath. It really did not help; it just made him a very soggy cat.

So there's never dull at either the back or front door at the ranch. Hope your doors open to excitement.

TTFN,
Mia

Off to the Vet

Howdy, all:

Since Peekaboo and the critters of the wild seem to have occasional get-togethers, it was time for him to get a rabies shot. (The skunk episode still being fresh in memory.)

So off to the vet. He traveled to the vet in a Bose speaker bag. He did produce *music* of the whining kind on the way. Now, why in a Bose speaker bag rather than the animal carrier? Well, last year, while running from the fires here in Central Texas, Phoenix, the other gray cat, had a "code brown" event in it. The carrier was no more.

And that is the story as to why Peekaboo went to the vet in a Bose bag.

Here at the ranch, music is made even in a pet carrier. May music be made in your world.

TTFN,
Mia

A Flock Has Arrived

Howdy, all:

Some blessed rain came over the weekend. And, with rain, came a flock of nine black-bellied whistling ducks. They are showing up on a regular basis to the backyard, visiting the birdseed found around the trees with birdfeeders in them.

The ducks flew in, whistling as they come, landed in the small area just outside the backyard, scouted the yard to check for any dangerous critters, and then marched in. They marched in a single file with an occasional hop to keep up with each other. Scouts were set up while the others ate. Then, the roles were reversed.

Wiggles came up to the edge of the backyard, held back by the electric fence, and watched the ducks gobbling down the food. Maybe Wiggles would like to join in the feeding party.

So all was *ducky* at the ranch. May your world also be ducky! (Couldn't resist!)

TTFN,
Mia

"Green Lips I have," Said Wiggles

Howdy, all:

One of the good things that have come from having a bit more rain this year is that the ponds have kept their water even the smallest of the three, Frog Pond.

However, Reflecting Pond, aka Pond of Despair, now has a coating on it. It is a green coating. Wiggles enjoys getting a drink from this pond. When she is done drinking, her lips are coated green. Aha, Cleopatra could not have had makeup this good!

So now, this pond has earned another name, Green Lips Pond. And that is how it is to be.

Green lips and makeup are now part of the ranch. May colorful decorations be part of your world.

TTFN,
Mia

Charge of the Cow Brigade

Howdy, all:

On this particular morning, the cows were making their way from the coastal pasture to the Big Muddy. With the herd, there are now three calves. Willy, the black-and-white longhorn has a black-and-white calf named JJ. Crazy Cow has a cute brown calf with a white face. Tweedle-Dee has a black calf with a white face.

The brown and black calves decided to nap in the pasture just behind the house. This area is between the house and the Big Muddy. The momma cows moved on to graze nearby.

Well, Wiggles wanted to check the new calves out. She walked over toward the napping calves when all of a sudden, Crazy Cow and Tweedle-Dee came to a-chargin'. Wiggles had to bolt to get out of their way. Oh, wee, those momma cows were not about to let Wiggles get close to their babies.

Here at the ranch, the charging continues. May you charge through your day.

TTFN,
Mia

The Running Fence Pony

Howdy, all:

On the ranch, one of the tasks is checking the status of the fences. This can be done on foot, via a golf cart, or more exciting on horseback. And Wiggles is a great horse to use for this task. Actually, Wiggles should be used as a Pony Express horse. She just loves to run and run. And being small and compact, she can "get up and go" very quickly.

Using her to check the fences is an adrenalin adventure. It may not be the most useful method because what Wiggles loves to do is race alongside the fences. So the checking of the fences is done at high speed. At least one can see that the fences are standing and, well, that is all that really matters, is it not?

The ranch fences are in decent condition So hopefully, any fences in your world are holding up.

TTFN,
Mia

The Cow Parade

Howdy, all:

Yesterday was filled with looking for a wayward coffee cup that had been dropped while riding a horse down Cardinal Lane. The search for the cup took a bit, for it seemed as if some animal had moved it. "Just what the world needs, caffeinated critters."

While hunting for the coffee cup, a cow parade was set up. This particular parade was making its way across the bridge. Dolly Madison was in the lead, and following closely behind her were all the calves, all five of them. Funny how they were all in a nice line as if directed to do so. Clara, the longhorn cow, anchored the parade.

The cows continued the parade up the slope toward the water trough and the salt lick, which they all enjoyed. The calves will sneak in a lick at the salt when the grown-up cows have had their fill.

From a search to a parade, all is well here at the ranch. May your day have a parade to enjoy.

TTFN,
Mia

The Tugly Woods

Howdy, all:

On the ranch, there are various horseback riding trails through the woods. When winds come along, these trails need some tending to, for trees and branches can block the trails.

There is one area of the ranch with a lot of dead and falling trees. This area has come to be known as the Tugly Woods. Hopefully, there is no Jabberwock residing there!

Two horseback riding trails go through this area: Junkyard Lane and Bones Trail. Junkyard Lane goes along the fence on the backside of one of the neighbors. And some of their old ranching equipment is stored along this fence line, hence the name for the trail. As for Bones Trail, there are quite a few bones from previous animals scattered about. Exactly why and how all these bones got to this area remains a mystery. Maybe one day, an answer will come.

At the ranch, all trails lead home. May your trail lead to your abode.

TTFN,
Mia

Peekaboo's Friend

Howdy, all:

The other morning, a mild morning, the front door was opened for Mr. Peekaboo to commence his morning promenade around the house. Miss Phoenix was lounging in the living room completely satiated from her morning breakfast. Now, you know that was going to change. And change it did.

Mr. Peekaboo came skittering into the house, jumped up on the dining room table, raced across it, dived into the red chair, and then raced back toward the front door. While all this was going on, there was a fluttering about the lamp over the dining room table. And then that fluttering headed toward the front door and out into the wild blue yonder.

Hmmm, Mr. Peekaboo had invited a bird friend into the house. And that bird friend had come and gone in a hurry. Poor Peekaboo, his only playmate was a lounging, satiated cat whose big activity was attacking the feed bowl.

Such is life at the ranch. Hope your life has a flutter or two in it.

TTFN,
Mia

A Little This, a Little That

Howdy, all:

On a drizzly morning, Peekaboo headed out to do his morning check around the house. He seemed to be tracking something down by the feed shed. Through the drizzle, two creatures appeared. At first, they looked like coyotes. Oh, no, Peekaboo, don't track coyotes! Thankfully, they were two deer. What a beautiful sight to see deer, playing in the pasture. They caught wind of our presence and flicked their white tails and disappeared into the woods. Meanwhile, Peekaboo made a dash back into the house. Maybe he had second thoughts of hunting deer!

There is a pair of wood ducks on Green Lips Pond. And, Mr. Roadrunner has made his home near the bend in the road down by the creek.

There are three new cows in the herd. Their names are Paintbucket, Dulce, and White Belly. For them, the green grass is poking its head out, and what a beautiful sight it is.

A little this and a little that on the ranch. May your world also have a bit of variety.

TTFN,
Mia

Here, Hold My Champagne Glass

Howdy, all:

Living in the country provides ample opportunity for cultured situations to arise. For example, the other evening, after extricating the old tires from the woods with the tractor and a chain, a use for the old tires had to be found. So why not use the tires as manure spreaders? But of course.

To spread the fun, no pun intended, why not hook the tires behind the pickup truck, put some champagne on ice, and say, "Hold my champagne glass and watch this?"

Now, you know, the neighbors, who were out working with their cattle, got quite a kick out of this scene. A pickup truck, with tires hooked behind it, was driving circles in the pasture on a balmy Texas eve. And don't say we are not cultured; we drank the champagne out of crystal glasses!

Life on the ranch is no drag. Hope your world is likewise.

TTFN,
Mia

A Birthday Celebration

Howdy, all:

Today, April 18, is Wiggles's fourth birthday. And déjà vu–like, it is a rainy and windy day. The day Wiggles was born was similar. But, right after her birth, biblical–like, the sun broke out shining, and Prince came dashing up to announce her birth. This stuff cannot be made up.

After her birth, Wiggles and her momma, Carry, were put in a small round pen with a shed for cover. Prince was outside the round pen to provide security.

And today, four years later, the horses came galloping toward the house when there was a break in the rain. They had been under the shed. For the birthday celebration, many carrots were given. After the treats, those three characters took off buckin', racin', and carryin' on with abandon.

Here at the ranch, carrots for all. And may a carrot treat be in your world today.

TTFN,
Mia

Hide-and-Seek

Howdy, all:

We had a wind and rain storm the other day. This does cause branches and trees to fall on the fences.

So the fence line must be checked.

One of the fences runs along the trail named Miniature Pony Lane. The path runs from behind the Big Muddy down to the creek. The neighbor has some miniature ponies, thus the name.

When the end of the trail was reached at the creek, a raccoon was noticed to be swimming upstream. What the heck was a raccoon doing swimming in the creek? He tried to hide in the brush alongside the creek, but his tail was hanging out. He seemed to want to get on with his business. Okay, onward Mr. Raccoon, take care of your chores!

Another mystery at the ranch. May your mysteries be good ones.

TTFN,
Mia

Purrfect Melody

Howdy, all:

The piano is in the dining area of the house. Peekaboo is not a fan of piano music. Whenever the ivories are to be *tickled*, he dashes to find a quiet spot.

Meanwhile, Phoenix padded over to the piano, climbed up the red chair next to it, clambered over onto the piano itself, and proceeded to hang her head over the keys. Intrigued by the moving keys, she slid down on top of them and played her own tune. It was a *Mozcat* tune, for sure!

So, *purrfect* melodies are happening here at the ranch. May your world likewise have beautiful sounds.

TTFN,
Mia

The Ranch Trifecta

Howdy, all:

In racing, the trifecta is "win, place, and show." In ranch life, it is, well, event number one, number two, and number three.

Event one: Wiggles has bronchitis. She must quit smoking the Pall Malls and eat nothing but filtered grass. She is on antibiotics in the hope that her cough will get better.

Event two: The new bull, Ferdinand, wanted to visit his paramour across the fence yesterday morning. Now, having a two-ton critter leaning on a fence does cause some problems. The cowboy owner had to come out and round up the cattle, along with a reluctant Ferdinand.

Event three: Carry was lying down during the cattle roundup in a funny position. Good Lord, she had colic. So she was gotten up and walked and walked and walked, hoping for some poop. Can you imagine praying for that? You see, colic can be fatal if the horse's colon becomes completely twisted. The horse has a "one-way" system. They cannot throw up. So, it must come out the other end.

After Carry was walked for a couple of hours and given medicine, she was loaded up and taken to the horse hospital. Thankfully, the colic had subsided. She was given some IV fluids to rehydrate her.

Whew, it's never dull with the ranch's trifecta. Hope your trifecta is less stressful.

TTFN,
Mia

The Mystery Egg

Howdy, all:

In early July of 2013, the Big Muddy dried completely up. An adventure of sorts happens when this occurs. One can see what is at the bottom of the pond. And, this particular time, a few stray golf balls were found in the drying mud.

The next day, the weeds around the pond were mowed so as to prevent them from taking over. Something white and round was sitting in the middle of the dried pond. Another golf ball? Well, gosh, it was not. It was a medium-sized egg. There were tracks about the egg, but what animal left its egg in the middle of a muddy, dried-up pond?

Here at the ranch, mysteries are being chalked up. Perhaps you have some mysteries in your world.

TTFN,
Mia

Whodunit

Howdy, all:

To help solve some of the mysteries here at the ranch, some of the local investigators are chatting back and forth with one another, sharing information. These *investigators* are the resident owls. The other day, there was an owl conference being held down by the creek.

Now, on the south side of the creek, Mr. Who was presiding. And on the north side of the creek, Mr. Whom was in charge. They were comparing their notes and *whooing* back and forth for quite some time.

It may be in the near future that we shall have some answers to our mysteries from Mr. Whom and Mr. Who. So stay tuned for further developments.

The ranch has its own investigators. May you have yours.

TTFN,
Mia

Guest at the Front Door

Howdy, all:

Yesterday, at the front door, lo and behold, there was Mr. Roadrunner. He must have figured out that the good stuff is kept inside the door! Actually, perhaps he was after the little gecko that makes its home in the plants by the front door.

Mr. Roadrunner took one look at the two-legged interloper, twitched his tail, turned, and dashed off. The gecko lives for another day.

You see, the gecko and Peekaboo have a "cat-and-gecko" game of hide-and-seek that is played most mornings. Perhaps Mr. Roadrunner had wanted to get in that game. Well, maybe next time he can join.

There are front-door surprises here at the ranch. Perhaps you, too, will have a surprise today.

TTFN,
Mia

The Summer of Discontent Is Finally Over

Howdy, all:

Boy, so glad this summer of discontent is over. All horses are back to whole and healthy. Wiggles is over her bronchitis; Carry, over her stomach infection and colic episode. Both horses are now on "Weight Loss for Equines" manufactured by Mr. Ed and Company!

Due to the drought, unused kitty litter boxes are being used as water buckets for the various animals on the ranch. But being the imp that she is, Wiggles has decided that these conveniently placed water "troughs" are for her. With a twinkle in her eye, because she knows she shouldn't, she drains the litter boxes with one, big, long gulp. Silly horse.

Does anyone want a scamp of a horse? The price will be right, for sure!

The summer of discontent is over, and all is as it should be here at the ranch. May your discontent be gone.

TTFN,
Mia

The Drought Continues

Howdy, all:

Even though the heat of the summer has passed, the rains have not come. So the creek is the gathering place for a lot of critters.

One of the animals staying close to the creek is a momma deer and her newborn fawn. They stay quite hidden in the woods that run along the creek. It was thought that some variety should be added to their diet. A head of cabbage was cut up and placed strategically for them. Now, one wonders, Do deer suffer from cabbage-induced flatulence? Inquiring minds want to know. Maybe Mr. Who and Mr. Whom can come up with an answer for all.

We hope for rain here at the ranch. Hope the needed moisture makes it to your world.

TTFN,
Mia

One and Two

Howdy, all:

With the fog lifting this morning, a *Tom and Jerry* scene played out in the yard. Peekaboo is out for his morning hunt. He finds a mouse. He starts *herding* the mouse, thankfully, away from the house. But the mouse, Mr. Monty, is not completely cooperating with Peekaboo's efforts. Monty stands on his hindlegs and gives Peekaboo first a right, then a left in the ol' kisser!

Peekaboo turns around and gives a look as if to say, "Did you see that?" Then, Monty scurries a few more paces, turns, and faces Peekaboo again. And once more, that mouse lands two good punches on Peekaboo's nose. Monty then disappears into a crevice in the ground. (It is so dry that the earth has cracks in it.)

Being a mouser at the ranch is a high-risk occupation, so with that, Mr. Peekaboo decides to go after the dove feeding at the birdfeeder.

A good ol' punch here and there sometimes happens at the ranch. May you stay clear of any!

TTFN,
Mia

Mystery Daddy Resolved

Howdy, all:

This morning, the mystery of what type of horse was Wiggles's daddy has been resolved. Which sire (a horse daddy) was father to Wiggles has been a matter of speculation ever since she was born. You see, her momma, Carry, was a rescue buy horse. And no information that she was pregnant was given at the time of the sale. So when Wiggles appeared, it really was as if a "two for one" had been gotten!

Now, back to solving the mystery. While Carry and Prince were lounging by the Memorial Garden, which is near the Big Muddy, the cows came up and started drinking from the pond. Wiggles was up on the bank of the Big Muddy, watching the cows drinking and splashing about. Well, obviously it was time for the cows to move on. So Wiggles charged down the bank and rounded all the cows up as if she was a highly trained cow pony. Her daddy, then, was a quarter horse. Just has to be.

So nice to solve a mystery at the ranch. May your day have a mystery solved.

TTFN,
Mia

The Four Moosketers

Howdy, all:

There are now four newborn calves; three are jet-black, and one is orange-and-white. These *mooskeers* form their own li'l gang.

While their mommas graze, they play. Many a mock battle is fought, new places explored, and *dares* are made. They seem to dare each other to get close to the "two-legged critter" that tramps about.

When they get close, they stop, look wide-eyed with a wide-legged stance, and any further motion toward the two-legged creature is really contemplated. If an unusual movement is made by that creature, the moosketer scampers off to the gang, and they all "high tail it" back toward their mommas. There they regain their courage and attempt another *dare* at the two-legged critter.

Ah, such is the life and the times of a moosketer!

At the ranch, many a dare is happening. Hope in your world, adventure awaits.

TTFN,
Mia

Color Schemes in the Cows

Howdy, all:

With balmy weather in Texas, the cows seem to be thriving. The new calves and their mommas are very content.

It is interesting what color each cow's calves are, considering that the bull, Ferdinand, is a solid black bull. For example, Clara is an orange-and-white longhorn, and her calf was black in color. Willie is a black-and-white longhorn, and her calf was brown-and-white. Hmmm. Now, Crazy Cow is black with a white face, and her calf is all black. Finally, Tweedle-Dee also had a calf that is black. Tweedle-Dee is black with some white on her belly.

So bets are being taken as to what color Vanilla's calf will be. (Yes, Vanilla is a white cow. Ferdinand is the daddy to be.)

Here at the ranch, the cow herd is a mix-and-match group. And hopefully, your world is likewise.

TTFN,
Mia

The Hum

Howdy, all:

Have you ever had one of those mornings where you hear something and, well, just cannot pin it down? Well, the other morning, there was a "hum" in the air. Looking up, looking down, where was this coming from? Peekaboo and Phoenix both scooted back into the house. They had been out the backdoor, catching some morning sun.

The "hum" got louder and more persistent. And then, a huge, and I mean *huge*, a flock of blackbirds came over the house, heading south. They must have just read "Birds" by Alfred Hitchcock! There were thousands of them, and apparently, the cold snap had caused them to join up with others to go south for the winter.

Once the flock passed overhead, the silence was restored. Quite amazing that birds in flight can cause such a racket.

All is quiet at the ranch now. May your day be peaceful.

TTFN,
Mia

The Running of the Cows

Howdy, all:

So the cold blast came in and with it, the winds knocked down some branches that fell on the road by the bridge. While picking up those branches, a snort was heard. Lo and behold, there was Clara, followed by Willie, followed by Ferdinand; and before you knew it, the whole entire cow herd was bearing down on the bridge! Oh, no, this cannot be Pamplona; this is Texas!

A single sapling was nearby. That sapling became cover from the running of the cows. They were hellbent on getting across the bridge and up to the Big Sandy Pasture. You see, the cowboy honks the truck horn, and the cows know it is the signal for special food—cow treats. They will make a mad dash to get those treats and woe to anything, anybody in their way. Just thank goodness the sapling provided a bit of cover from the stampede!

It is never dull at the ranch. And hopefully, in your world, you get no bull. (Couldn't resist!)

TTFN,
Mia

From Dobbin to Wiggles

Howdy, all:

The search for the saddle I used as a "Pippi Longstocking" youngster has come to a successful end. I found the saddle my father had bought me many, many ago. I used this saddle to ride my faithful first steed, Dobbin. Dobbin, in my mind, was as "fast as the wind," and she and I used to race many a semitruck struggling to get up the hill from the valley near the home place. Of course, Dobbin always won, and the truckers always gave a *toot* to salute the victor.

Now that very same saddle, restored to good condition, graces Wiggles. Today was the inaugural ride, and although the saddle had a creak or two, Wiggles raced the wind and won. (With the crowd roaring, actually, it was the birds scattering.)

Here at the ranch, tradition lives on. May in your world, a tradition holds.

TTFN,
Mia

Horse Ballet

Howdy, all:

On this frosty Texas morning, the three horses were out in the back pasture. Prince decided that a little ballet was in order to warm them up.

So he nuzzled Carry; she pirouetted. Then, Prince and Carry posed, nose to nose, and with hooves pointed. Prince broke that pose and headed to Wiggles. He and Wiggles stretched their necks out, and then both leaped into the air, a cabriolet pose with tails outstretched.

Next came the synchronized movement to the feed shed. Prince got behind Carry, and she started moving forward. Prince then nuzzled Wiggles, and she stepped in line with him, and in a coordinated pace-forpace motion, the three horses danced toward the feed shed.

The ducks were in the backyard feeding; however, they stopped long enough to *quack* their approval at this performance.

The dance of life continues at the ranch. May your day have a step or two in it.

TTFN,
Mia

The Horse Sit-In

Howdy, all:

Mornings at the ranch are a bit like Christmas. When the light of day comes, and one looks out, it is always with a bit of anticipation as to "what will the light reveal?"

The other morning, as the sun made its way, what was revealed was Carry, lying down just outside the front door area, waiting for her morning feed. Her pose stated: "You are late. I am waiting for my food. Where are you? Hurry up." Believe me, Mr. Ed could not have spoken more loudly and plainly.

Prince and Wiggles were standing guard about her as if they were large bookends. Everything must wait until the starving horses are fed. Hmmm.

Here at the ranch, the light of day brought a message. May your day have a message brought to you.

TTFN,
Mia

Mistletoe Hunting

Howdy, all:

Mistletoe adorns a few of the trees around the house. Last year, a ladder and a lot of physical effort went into removing as much of this parasite from the trees as possible.

This year, however, a new plan of attack was hatched. Why not shoot the mistletoe out of the trees? So that is what was done.

I must admit, it sure was a lot of fun, trying to hit the stalk that connected the mistletoe to the tree branch. Even with the wind swaying the trees, a fair number of the mistletoe clumps were knocked out of the trees.

So I wonder if this could be a business one could promote? "Shooters of Mistletoe" at your service!

Here at the ranch, the nonsense continues. Here's hoping you have a little nonsense in your world.

TTFN,
Mia

Sloth as an Art Form

Howdy, all:

Phoenix, the gray cat rescued from the middle of the highway, has perfected the art of sloth. She can lounge with the best of them.

After her morning meal, she strolls languidly to the sunny portion of the garage. There she sprawls herself on the blue rug, soaking up the morning rays. Then, after her midday meal, she meanders onto one of the beds. And there she plops herself smack dab in the middle of the bed. If it is a cool day, she finds the heating pad and looks at you imploringly to turn it on. But only on low, please.

Later, after the evening meal, she crawls up onto a convenient lap and flops down with the authority of a presidential paperweight, allowing minimal movement until her midnight snack. Botticelli could not have had a better model for his paintings than Miss Phoenix.

Here at the ranch, lounging is an art. May you have a bit of relaxation in your world.

TTFN,
Mia

Ol' Man Winter's Gift

Howdy, all:

Ol' Man Winter visited Central Texas yesterday and brought rain that became sleet that became icy rain.

This morning, Mr. Winter's gift was the painting of every shrub, tree, fence wire, and grass blade with shimmering ice. And how beautiful it was with the sun peeking out, making everything sparkle.

Prince and Wiggles cavorted about like circus horses. They reared on the hind legs, pranced about, and raced after one another. All the while, Carry was happily munching away.

When their game was completed, they trotted over to Carry; Prince was on one side of her, Wiggles on the other. They reached their noses across Carry's back and teased each other. After a few minutes of this, Carry lifted her head long enough to look first at Prince and then at Wiggles as if to say, "Enough, children. Enough." With that, all three horses settled in the corner of the coastal pasture and happily munched away on the sparkling grass.

There is some sparkle here at the ranch. May your world have a few shiny things in it too.

TTFN,
Mia

The Afternoon Matinee

Howdy, all:

Today, Mr. Tom Turkey gave a demonstration of the correct *turkey-trot* technique. He was showing Mrs. Thomasina Turkey the finer intricacies of this dance. He did include the fanning of the feathers akin to a very good flamenco dancer. Wonderful.

This afternoon's performance took place in the Big Sandy Pasture. Some of the spectators of this matinee were Wiggles, Prince, and Carry. They were truly engaged and fascinated by this dance.

And it might be added that Mr. Tom did this in the shade of a very nice cedar tree. He does try and take care to not burn his wattle in the Texas sun.

Stay tuned for future performances. Tickets are available.

Matinees at the ranch. May your day have a show worth watching.

TTFN,
Mia

In the Eye

Howdy, all:

Well, Wiggles got a scratch in her eye. From what is a mystery.

The scratch was not healing, and getting medication into a horse's eye is a challenge. So Ms. Wiggles is at the horse hospital. (Cards and carrots will be accepted.) She has an IV in the eye, and medication is being directly put into the eye. Amazing what can be done. Her mane is braided with the IV line in it. That part looks cute. The hope is that she will not lose her sight in that eye. We would have to rename her "Cyclops."

Prince and Carry are searching for her. When they see the neighbor's cows, they whinny and nay until they figure out they are cows and not Wiggles.

Ms. Wiggles should be in the horse hospital for about a week.

Here's hoping the trio of horses is reunited soon here at the ranch. May your world be all together also.

TTFN,
Mia

The Lesson of Patience

Howdy, all:

Wiggles is still in the horse hospital, still receiving medications via the IV tube to her eye.

Did you know there was such a profession as a horse eye surgeon? Well, Wiggles had a consult with a horse eye surgeon. Imagine that.

There is a pus pocket right on her cornea. It would involve a very delicate surgery to remove it, and there would be scarring right in the middle of her cornea.

So it has been determined that more time and more medicine are needed to see if eventually, the blood supply will reach that pocket and the infection be dealt with the medications, rather than surgically removing it. Patience is the key.

The ranch life is learning the healing of time. May time give your world healing.

TTFN,
Mia

Two Eyes Is Horse

Okay, Wiggles remains at the hospital. There is a *war* going on in her eye. Her eye is red, full of blood vessels. So now, we wait and hope that her system and the medicines defeat the infection. The horse eye doctor saw her on Tuesday and said these next few days are critical. If the infection cannot be fought off, then the eye will need to be removed. Her name will be changed to *Wyclops*. Hmm.

Her stall mates at the hospital really whinny and carry on when she is taken out for a walk. She has made friends with her fellow equine eye patients.

As to the rest of the ranch, there has been a sighting of a beautiful gray fox. The turkeys and ducks continue to come to the backyard for their feed. And we pray for rain.

Prince and Carry have gotten a bit fat without Wiggles to chase them. She was always getting them to play.

The *eyes* have it at the ranch. May you see all in your world.

TTFN,
Mia

Eat Your Carrots

Howdy, all:

According to the horse eye doctor, Wiggles is "winning the war" with the eye infection, and at this time, removal of the eye does not look necessary. Credit for this turnaround is being given to the carrots she gets! Yeah, for beta carotene!

And soon, Wiggles will return to the ranch and see that she has new mates—there are some new cows. They are Brahma cows. Their names are Doe, Bambi, Caspar, and Methusela. They are quite a sight for sure.

Carrots for all here at the ranch. Be sure to get your dose in your world.

TTFN,
Mia

Phidippides

Howdy, all:

There is a caracara, or a Mexican eagle, that appears to be injured. He cannot fly. He is full grown and has made his home in the Big Sandy Pasture. There, he hunts the moles. He hops over to one of their mounds, cocks his head to listen, and then uses his powerful legs to dig and secure himself a meal.

Since he cannot fly, he *runs* and uses the cedar trees in the pasture as his refuge. Thus, he is Phidippides, named after the first runner of the "Marathon."

As to the other critters, Wiggles remains at the horse hospital but should be coming home this next week. Now, won't that be a celebration? Can you imagine all the whinnyin' and snortin' and carryin' on that will take place when she is reunited with Prince and Carry.

Things are running along here at the ranch. May your world run smoothly.

TTFN,
Mia

A Miracle

Howdy, all:

Glad to report that Wiggles is back home. The IV is still in her eye, and she is still receiving IV meds twice a day (ten more days).

But the vets are astounded by her progress, and it appears that not only is her eye saved, but she does also retain some vision in it. Previously, vision was considered not possible in this eye.

Now she and Carry are enjoying afternoon grazing, and at night, she has her own little pen. Prince is being kept on the outside of the horse pasture because he is *mad* at Wiggles for being gone so long. Until Wiggles's IV catheter comes out, he will be on his own during the day.

Oh, it appears as if Phidippides has some ability to fly. Maybe his injury is healing. But he is doing a good job clearing the moles from the Big Sandy Pasture. Yeah.

Here's to miracles at the ranch. May a miracle come your way.

TTFN,
Mia

Gone to the Birds

Howdy, all:

The birds have it at the ranch. For example, the black-bellied whistling ducks have had some babies. They are very, very shy. The babies are kept well-hidden near the Big Muddy.

The turkeys have had some *turkets*. And they wander into the yard, ducking under the electric fence and having a snack at the birdseed.

And Phidippides, the Mexican eagle, continues to make his home in the horse pasture. (He moved from the Big Sandy Pasture to the horse pasture last week.) He occasionally gets a snack of "buckshot snake" and seems to enjoy it very much. He also has earned his own water bucket.

Wiggles, Prince, and Carry watch this parade of birds. Yesterday evening, the turkey parade went among the horses and cows. Wiggles watched them carefully. (Her vision seems to improve daily.)

Birds, birds, and more birds here at the ranch. May your thoughts take wing.

TTFN,
Mia

Time for Babies

Howdy, all:

It is truly the time for babies—the four-legged type.

The new herd of cows, Brahma cows and Ferdinand, the black bull, and a new bull in the making—a Hereford named Henry—have started their "baby business." Loretta, a Brahma cow whose color is that of soot (thus, Loretta, the coal miner's daughter), has a brindle calf. That means it has stripes like a tiger.

Bambi, a fawn-colored Brahma cow, has had an all-white calf with long, floppy ears and very long legs. It has earned the name of "Galloping Goat."

Tweedle-Dum., a black cow with a white face, has had an all-black calf. Okay, "Blackie?" And all eyes are on Ninety-Nine, a young cow that is due soon. Her ear tag is number ninety-nine.

Phidippides continues to patrol the horse pasture. He has become a welcome fixture to the menagerie.

Life continues here at the ranch. And hope, likewise, a new generation blooms in your world.

TTFN,
Mia

D and T

Howdy, all:

The latest in the parade of wildlife are the deer and now fourteen turkeys.

There are five deer: one momma with twin fawns and another with one fawn. The momma deer with the twin waits each morning for the sound of the golf cart. She knows that corn will be coming when she hears the cart. She and her twins have made their home in the glen just east of the Big Sandy Pasture. The other momma and fawn are more elusive. They occasionally wander in from the neighbor's woods to feast on the corn treats.

Now, the turkeys continue to multiply. This morning, the parade through the backyard was a total of fourteen! They shoo the ducks away from the food. Quite funny to see a turkey chasing a duck!

So, the *D*'s and *T*'s continue to add to the ranch. May your world have some interesting additions.

TTFN,
Mia

Rain and Penelope

Howdy, all:

Big news! We received two inches of rain yesterday. Woohoo!

The next item, Phidippides, the caracara or Mexican eagle, has a girlfriend. Her name is Penelope. She is patient and waits for Phidippides as he skitters across the pasture while she gracefully glides above.

They share the hamburger meat and hot dogs left for them.

The poop fence is to hold the cows at bay. A line of cow manure has been placed around the young trees lining the road, and this fence has been keeping the cows from munching on those trees.

Mr. Roadrunner has been a regular in the backyard. He even has ventured onto the back porch.

Patience is rewarded here at the ranch. May your patience also be rewarded.

TTFN,
Mia

I Can Fly! I Can fly!

Howdy, all:

Guess what, Phidippides can fly. Indeed, he can. Ah, the power of hot dogs and hamburger meat!

The other day, Phidippides was at his tree, eating his hamburger snack. Penelope was waiting in a nearby tree. After he had his snack, he took a running start, and voila, he took off. What a sight, and what a miracle to see him back in flight. His hurt wing appears to have healed.

Prior to this successful takeoff, he had been hanging around in the trees, flying short distances. He was working up the courage for this big flight. Yeah.

We have now received over five inches of rain. The grass has started to turn green again.

Here at the ranch, we are all flyin' high. Hope you can soar to new heights.

TTFN,
Mia

Acornucopia

Howdy, all:

Prince found a batch of acorns under an oak tree in the horse pasture the other day. And acorns and horses do not get along. Acorns have been known to cause a horse to founder, which means the horse becomes lame.

So to keep Prince from eating the acorns, some panels were moved from the round pen to fence off the acorn feasting area. Well, Prince followed this effort very closely. He snorted and looked at what was being done, tossed his head about, and then wheeled around and raced out of the pasture.

His acorn feast came to an abrupt end.

Sometimes the feasting must stop here at the ranch. And, likewise, in your world, it also must stop.

TTFN,
Mia

Quack Bulova

Howdy, all:

Okay, stand aside, Bulova, Timex, and so on. Black-bellied whistling ducks can tell the time. In fact, one can set one's clock to them.

You see, ladies and gents, the ducks come in at 7:30 a.m. They announce their arrival. Better sound than any ol' alarm clock around—except maybe the bacon-sizzlin'.

And in the afternoon, they come in for their snack promptly at 4:30 p.m. Again, they announce their arrival.

So who needs a clock? Just get yourself a flock of these ducks, and you can free yourself of the *ticktock*.

Here at the ranch, time is quacked. (Couldn't resist!) May time be delightfully announced in your world.

TTFN,
Mia

The Rescue

Howdy, all:

The turkeys, all fifteen of them, showed back up. Since Thanksgiving is over, they figured it was safe to come back!

Speaking of Thanksgiving, a rescue happened that just must be recorded.

Melanie (a sister of mine) and I were whizzing on the golf cart, feeding the critters along the lane. We did not see the horses until we were returning home. Prince met us at the top of the rise on the far side of the creek. He would not let me pet him. He kept backing down the hill, seemingly wanting us to follow him. Wiggles was munching at the bottom of the hill. Carry was nowhere to be seen.

Prince would move forward a few steps, never letting us get close enough to pet him, and when we did approach him, he would back up some more, making sure we were following. With him leading us, we went down Bird Trail and onto the north end of 'Telephone Pole Trail. There in the brambles was Carry. She was caught by her neck and legs. She was caught by the spiny vines. Thankfully, she stood very still while we untangled her.

Thanks to Prince, Carry was rescued without a scratch on her. He sure was her prince!

Giving thanks here at the ranch. May you have gratitude in your world.

TTFN,
Mia

The "Brave" New World

Howdy, all:

There in the backyard were fifteen of the biggest turkeys one could ever see. Mr. Peekaboo saw them. He went out the backdoor and headed off to investigate these big birds. Just as soon as the turkeys saw Peekaboo, they came a runnin' toward him. He quickly retreated under one of the chairs on the back porch. The turkeys clucked about, just beyond the back patio, eyeing Peekaboo as only turkeys can eye.

This turkey standoff lasted about ten minutes. Then, one of the lead turkeys decided they had had enough, and off went the turkey brigade to inspect the front yard for more critters to chase.

Mr. Peekaboo emerged from his hiding place and sauntered back into the house with the stride stating, "I really showed 'em." Hmm.

Bravery on display at the ranch. May your world have the fearless in it.

TTFN,
Mia

We Get the Good Stuff

Howdy, all:

Well, Prince has done it again. His personality has really blossomed this year. This is what recently happened.

A bale of coastal hay that was not good quality was given to the cows rather than to the horses. A good bale with a sprinkling of alfalfa was set out for the horses.

The lesser quality of coastal hay was spread out for the cows. Prince was intently watching this. He was standing as if "on guard" at the top of the hill. He came over to the piles for the cows and inspected them to make sure that they were not getting the "good stuff."

After his inspection was done, he trotted back up the hill and to his gals and his feed. Before eating, he gave a look as if to say, "Just wanted to make sure they weren't getting any of our feed."

So here at the ranch, ya get the good stuff. Make sure you are getting the good food in your world.

TTFN,
Mia

Wild Kingdom

Howdy, all:

Perhaps some of you remember the TV show the *Wild Kingdom*, hosted by Mutual of Omaha. That show could have been shot here at the ranch the other day.

The scene went like this. Early morning brought all the fifteen turkeys to the backyard to eat. All of a sudden, they moved very rapidly to the north side of the house. What could have caused this? Well, a scraggly, small coyote had shown up. He was not even as big as the turkeys. He was stalking the turkeys. The turkeys lined up with the necks craned and eyes trained on his movements. He saw the odds and snuck back into the woods.

The next morning, all fifteen showed back up. Guess Mr. Coyote is still hunting.

The hunt goes on here at the ranch. May you have good hunting in your world.

TTFN,
Mia

The Ranch Derby

Howdy, all:

The other day, the farrier came out to trim the horses' hooves. As usual, the horses decided to *hide* from the farrier. (Reminds me of someone who used to hide from the piano teacher. Hmm.)

Anyway, they were in the Tugly Wood by Junkyard Lane. So I went up with the feed bucket and tried to entice them to come rather than me having to lead them up. Oh, no, they knew an empty feed bucket when they heard one. All right, then, I had to get some carrots, real carrots.

With that, Wiggles started following me. Prince and Carry followed. When we reached the bridge, I drove across (I was in the golf cart) and waited for them to cross. Wiggles, then Carry, and finally, Prince came across. Wiggles waited for Prince and Carry to get slightly ahead of her, and then the race was on. The ranch derby was being run! Tails and manes a *flyin*! Up the hill, the racers went. Care to bet which horse won?

Here at the ranch, the race is run. May your race be successful in your world.

TTFN,
Mia

Odds and Ends

Howdy, all:

The other day, a large flock of snow geese were flying due north. Their honking gave them away. However, almost as if the great "Traffic Director in the Sky" had put up a turn sign, the flock took a hard right turn and started flying east. It was the cold front that was sweeping in that they *ran into.*

Mr. Tom Turkey comes most days to feast on the birdseed in the backyard. He is a tall chap and yet is quite nimble at ducking under the electric fence that goes 'round the house.

The black-bellied whistling ducks are "on again, off again" visitors. Why their regular twice-a-day feedings have become irregular is a mystery. Perhaps our cold weather has something to do with it.

And finally, the elusive deer, three does, seem to have settled in the forest by the creek. If one is lucky, they can be spotted. However, their tracks are quite regular on the trails. They are known as "Doe, Ray, Mi." Now, ain't that cute?

Here at the ranch, we have some odds and ends. Hopefully in your world, the odds and ends contribute goodness.

TTFN,
Mia

Mr. Wily E. Coyote and the *Horskey*

Howdy, all:

This day started out as all early spring days. Birds were flying in for food, horses begging for treats, and Mr. Turkey making his way through it all.

Mr. Turkey ate his fill of birdseed. He then proceeded down to the horse pasture, oh, excuse me, the turkey pasture where he tried to get Carry's attention with his mating dance. She could not have been less interested. Eating green grass was more exciting than producing a *horskey*.

In the midst of his flirtations with Carry, his feathers suddenly fell. Rejection, well, no. Coyote, yes. Mr. Wily E. Coyote was slinking along the back fence. Turkey fritters were on his mind. Well, with this sighting, Mr. Turkey "turned tail and ran." He ran all the way down to the creek. Mr. Coyote slunk back into the woods, and Carry kept grazing.

It's never dull at the ranch. Hope your day has a touch of excitement.

TTFN,
Mia

The Weight Watcher Trifecta

Howdy, all:

Due to the blessings of our spring rains, the grass is greener on both sides of the fence, and the horses have gotten a little fat, shall we say.

So today started the Weight Watcher Trifecta. That is, ride one horse and have all follow and get a good bit of exercise. Carry, being the "Boss Momma," is the one to ride. Prince and Wiggles will follow her.

And that is how it went today. Carry whinnied for them to follow. If she had to move, they had to move. Prince and Wiggles came to a *runnin'*. Carry was in high cotton, leading the parade. Her head was high, her gait was smooth and brisk, and she kept Wiggles from passing her. Wiggles was trying to take the lead. Carry would have none of it. Just like a petulant teenager, Wiggles then turned her attention to teasing and cavorting with Prince. Prince is so patient with her antics.

The ride came to an end, and all three had worked up a bit of sweat. Carry gave the swish of her tail that now it was time for her to get some carrots. Carrots are on the Weight Watcher's diet, aren't they?

Can't lose for winning at the ranch. May your world suffer no losses.

TTFN,
Mia

Whoops

Howdy, all:

Just this morning, watching the flights of the black-bellied whistling ducks in and out, there was a *whoops* moment.

The ducks have been taken to perching in a dead tree by the Big Muddy. I think this must be a lookout, posting for the flock swimming on the Big Muddy. Anyway, there also is a dead tree near the backyard. Two ducks took off from their feasting and headed to this nearby tree. Simultaneously, they landed on one branch. Well, the branch broke. *Whoops* went the ducks, flapping their wings to regain flight from this mishap.

And then there is the "Lonely Hearts Club" Mr. Tom Turkey. Ever since his failed courtship of Carry, he has been a regular to the backyard, asserting his claim to the food. In fact, the other day, he was quite upset that I was taking so long to mow the lawn. He was giving me the "stink eye" and stomping his feet sending the clear message that I needed to hurry along with my mowing. Now, exactly who is the boss around this joint?

All is well at the ranch even with whoops and impatient turkeys. Have a good whoop in your world.

TTFN,
Mia

A Surprise Visitor

Howdy, all:

A surprise visitor came to the ranch over the weekend. Miss Fiona flew in from California to watch her brother march in his Texas A and M "final review" for his freshman year.

Fiona decided to step up to the challenge and ride Wiggles. Now, Wiggles is a small, compact, but powerful horse. And riding her is a bit like riding "four sticks of dynamite." One must be up to the challenge. And the jury is in; Miss Fiona is up to the challenge. She galloped and rode Wiggles like a champ and had Wiggles literally eating out of her hand.

But that is not all Fiona accomplished on her visit to the ranch. She proceeded to finish naming the cows. Some of the cows now have names such as Pralines n' Cream, Oreo, Cookies and Cream, Peanut, Skippy, Swiss Miss, and so forth. Is a theme noted in these names? The cows are enjoying their new-found identities and just keep munchin' on.

Treats and all here at the ranch. May your world have some treats in it too.

TTFN,
Mia

Mysteries

Howdy, all:

Over the past week or so, there have been a number of mysteries—all of them unsolved.

First mystery: A duck egg appeared in the backyard. Just one egg. And why was it there? The ducks have never laid their eggs in the backyard. They just eat and cavort about.

Second mystery: A flock of hawks, Cooper's hawks, was spotted over a section of the coastal pasture. Have you ever heard of a flock of hawks?

Third mystery: A lone Muscovy duck is now showing up in the mornings. He has a white head and breast area and black wings. He is quite a bit larger than the whistling ducks.

Final mystery: A lone deer showed up yesterday evening. Not once, but twice. Will she show up again?

Sherlock Holmes is needed here at the ranch. Hope your mysteries are solved.

TTFN,
Mia

Deer Chaser by James Fenimore Peekaboo

Howdy, all:

The backyard is Peekaboo's, and with his permission, the ducks, turkeys, rabbits, and squirrels can come and feast. However, he draws the line at deer.

Have you ever seen a cat chase a deer? He puffs himself up to three times his size, puts on his racing shoes, and darts out lickety-split after the deer. Doris the Deer turns and sees the ball of white-and-orange hurtling toward her, and with one graceful bound, she clears the electric fence and heads toward the Big Muddy. Once she clears the yard, Mr. Peekaboo is satisfied that he has once again taken charge of his backyard.

Doris has started coming a bit later in the evening after Peekaboo has retired indoors. She is no fool.

The chase is on here at the ranch. May your chase be fruitful.

TTFN,
Mia

The Creature from the Black Lagoon

Howdy, all:

Although there really is not a black lagoon at the ranch, there is a creek that runs year-round. And the other evening, on the way to saddle the horses was a sight in the middle of the road near the creek. A huge turtle was lying in the middle of the new gravel by the bridge.

Upon inspection, it was ancient-looking, with a soft shell. The head was very angular. And it retreated into its shell when approached.

It was determined best to leave the creature where it was and go for the evening ride. Upon return after the ride, the turtle was gone. But a four-to-five inch perfectly round hole had been dug in the gravel. For now, that hole is marked with a big rock so as to protect it. It may be a nest for eggs.

A little research revealed that this particular turtle is a Texas spiny softshell turtle. Hmm.

More critters at the ranch than you can shake a stick at. May your world be also so populated.

TTFN,
Mia

Comings and Goings

Howdy, all:

Summertime is in full swing here at the ranch. Hot and dry. The animals are coming and going. It goes like this.

The ducks keep coming. In fact, they have laid a few more eggs in the backyard. However, the lone Muscovy duck has not come back for the last two weeks.

The turkeys have not been seen for some time. A lone one was sighted about a week ago. But, otherwise, they are absent.

Doris the Deer came up about a week ago with a new friend, Dorothy the Deer. They retreat during the hot hours to the cool woods.

Spiny, the prehistoric soft-shelled turtle, has headed upstream to finish her egg-laying process. Maybe there will be more turtles soon.

The summer life continues here at the ranch. May your summer be full of life.

TTFN,
Mia

Life and Death on the Ranch

Howdy, all:

Some time ago, Paint Tail, one of the new Brahma cows, was being loaded up for sale, and she had a heart attack and died. The story goes that she died of a broken heart, leaving this Bovine paradise.

Then, a few weeks ago, two raccoons were found dead for no apparent reason. A bit of research found that Mother Nature has her own way of keeping the raccoon population in check. It is called a distemper.

But life continues in other realms. Shadrach, Meshach, and Abednego, the three rabbits living around the house, are thriving. Especially since a certain sinister, slithery critter was shot into hawk food.

Mr. Toad occupies Toad Hall, formerly known as the Well House. Mr. Frog is living on the back porch, much to Peekaboo's delight.

The circle of life continues here at the ranch. And, it probably is the same in your world.

TTFN,
Mia

Facelift, Ranch Style

Howdy, all:

The Vita Salon has come to the ranch, and a facelift has been taking place.

The first upgrade has been to the Memorial Garden. Beautiful red mulch is now outlining the garden. Next, the gate at the end of the lane has been given a coat of fresh black paint. The tractor is now a beautiful sky-blue color, having received its own new paint job. And the faded blue color of the Well House is being covered by a fresh coat of grass-green paint.

And finally, Mother Nature has done the best job ever. She gave us an inch of rain and the grass is a lustrous green. The sage plants have also exploded with brilliant purple flowers. The honeybees are in *bee heaven*.

The ranch is being revitalized. May your world receive the same.

TTFN,
Mia

It's Mine

Howdy, all:

Ralph the Roadrunner has claimed the Memorial Garden as his. (Reminds me of the seagulls in *Finding Nemo*—"mine, mine, mine!")

The other day, putting out birdseed around the St. Francis statue that graces the Garden, Ralph stood on the split rail fence, hopping about as if to say, "Mine, mine, mine," and I should leave his garden. He was busy chasing insects, geckos, and the like, and I was interrupting his work!

This morning, a wood duck again joined the noisy and rambunctious black-bellied whistling ducks for their morning feed. His plumage is so strikingly beautiful.

Doris the Deer peeked into the noisy backyard to see what all was going on. She decided it was much too noisy to have a morning snack.

One's claim is guarded here at the ranch. May your claim in life be also protected.

TTFN,
Mia

Prince's Trip

Howdy, all:

Here at the ranch, things have been hopping. The other afternoon, Prince did not eat his alfalfa snack. Rather, he *gummed* it and then walk away and just stood with his head bowed. His respiratory rate was rapid, and he had a fever. His breath was putrid.

Being that he is the "old man" of the group, he was taken to the horse hospital. There he was tested, treated, and stayed for a couple of days for observation.

He is home now, on an antibiotic, and has reestablished his primacy in the feeding routine. He has the "girls," the "Brown Sisters" (Carry and Wiggles are both brown-colored horses), in their rightful place.

Thank goodness he has appeared to make a full recovery. The vet came out for a follow-up visit, and he is doing well. So his trip to the hospital was a good one, short and sweet and back home.

Here at the ranch, we are hoping all trips are good ones. And may your trips be the same.

TTFN,
Mia

I, Peekaboo

Howdy, all:

"I, Peekaboo, alone, yet valiantly, defended the food line in the backyard from the invasion of the five deer. I stood my ground, twitched my tail, puffed up my fur, and had those dastardly deer out of my yard before you could shake a can of cat food.

"From now on, my title is 'Peekaboo the Pugnacious.' Pay no attention to the fact that the turkeys chase me into the house. That is a very minor detail. I am the 'deer slayer,' and the birdseed and deer corn (oh, another minor detail) are safe for those quacking, noisy, raucous ducks that I do not have time to chase."

The ranch is safe from any invasion of deer. Does that not make one feel that all is right with the world?

Here's to the abode at the ranch being secure from such threatening critters as Doris and her offspring. May your deer slayer in your world be as mindful.

TTFN,
Mia

Boo Careful What You Wish For

Howdy, all:

The wish has been for more rain. Well, for Halloween, Mother Nature decided to revisit an earlier chapter in the history of man, the replay of "Noah's Ark."

So last weekend, we received eight inches in about thirty-six hours. Minor flooding. Most of that water was soaked into the very dry soil. Okay, and on Halloween, Mother Nature wanted to really *scare us*. Ten inches in four hours. How about that for dunking apples?

The road into the ranch has been sculpted into gravel drifts and canyons. Fence lines have been rearranged. And the Big Muddy is really the Big Muddy.

So "boo" careful as to what you wish for. Mother Nature may oblige. And in your world, hope Mother Nature does not provide too much of a scare.

TTFN,
Mia

Where for Art Thou, Stumpy

Howdy, all:

A certain critter by the name of Stumpy made his presence felt recently. Mr. Stumpy is a feral hog. And he thought it would be a good idea to plow up the backyard and plant a garden, perhaps a garden of corn.

Well, the vegetable garden idea may be a good one, and I sure am appreciative of his efforts to "help me!" get the garden going; but really, since veggie gardens don't grow chocolate, I am not enthusiastic about the idea.

Now that the backyard has been somewhat put back in place and the electric fence repaired, Mr. Stumpy has disappeared. "Where for art thou, Stumpy?" We may need some ribs for Thanksgiving.

Here's to your garden of life. May it grow your hearts' delight.

TTFN,
Mia

A Return by Rebel?

Howdy, all:

After the Halloween flood, a cow from the neighbors made her way over the fence that was damaged by the flood. That cow was Rebel. She enjoyed a couple of days grazing the ranch with no competition from her herd.

Well, her rebel ways had to be redirected through the gap gate at the end of the coastal pasture back to her herd. All seemed fine. But this morning, a frosty morning, Rebel was standing at the gap gate looking longingly over. Her thoughts were probably centered around, *Where can I get over this fence?* Hmmm. Time will tell if Rebel makes her return.

Meanwhile, the riding trails are back "up and running." Wiggles tested them out this morning and gave 'em hooves upgrade.

Here's to your inner rebel. May it run on the wild side (once in a while!).

TTFN,
Mia

Pepe le Peu, Stand Aside!

Howdy, all:

In the midst of a lazy morning, an event caught Peekaboo's olfactory sense. Now, picture this, Phoenix, the Botticelli cat model, comes waddling out, heads for the front garden, roots about in the garden, and, in the process, takes care of the call of Mother Nature.

Peekaboo was sitting quietly, flicking his tail, surveying his kingdom, when the waft from Phoenix's *business* struck him. He let out a cat yelp, jumped up onto the wooden bench, and from there to the windowsill. He sat there looking down on the "olfactory offender" with all the disdain a cat can muster.

Meanwhile, oblivious to the vapor she had emitted, Phoenix lumbers over to a sunny part of the porch and sprawls out, preening herself in obvious satisfaction. Peekaboo remained on his perch until the olfactory coast was clear.

Sitting upwind may be the best policy at the ranch. And probably, likewise, in your world.

TTFN,
Mia

Jemima Puddle Duck at the Bridge

Howdy, all:

There is a new resident at the ranch. Jemima Puddle Duck has moved in at the bridge. She is a big Muscovy duck. And for some reason, she has taken up residence at the bridge.

She has instituted a toll for crossing "her bridge." It is a handful of corn. And it can either be put on the bridge in a nice little pile, or it can be tossed down into the shallow edges of the creek. Either way will get you across the bridge without a *fine*. The fine is a "duck stare down." Have you ever had a big duck stare at you with a steady gaze? Shiver me timbers, it causes me to tremble!

Santa Claus did come to the ranch. Three of his "reindeer" were resting in the backyard on Christmas Eve. (This is no Texas tall tale, either!) It had to be Comet, Dasher, and Prancer.

It's a little "corny" here at the ranch to cross the bridge. (Couldn't resist!) Hope your world has little nonsense in it.

TTFN,
Mia

Wake Up and Smell the Turkey

Howdy, all:

Sometimes waking up suddenly and looking out the window is not always the best idea. The other day, staring back at me were fifteen big turkeys. Those long necks were craning about looking in the window and bobbing up and down as they searched for food. They sure got my blood going!

This gang of turkeys has been, recently, regular visitors to the ranch. They seem to really enjoy the handful of corn offerings they find at the bridge that are intended for Jemimah. As for Jemimah, she does not appreciate their presence, especially their eating of her toll corn. She twitches her tail in duck disgust at their noisy gobbling and, no pun intended, their gobbling of her food.

Here at the ranch, all must find their own place. Hope you can find your own spot in your world.

TTFN,
Mia

Turkey Burst

Howdy, all:

Last week, Wiggles and I went for a ride. We went down Cardinal Lane. And there we ran into the Gobbler Gang, the fifteen turkeys who now "rule the roost."

Needless to say, Wiggles was a bit tense. I mean, these turkeys are fairly good-sized birds. They were on the trail, strutting about and clucking to one another. No telling what was going to happen.

I sat tight in the saddle and just waited to see what these gobblers would do. Wiggles had her *guard* up also. In an instant, all fifteen turkeys burst into the air, going in fifteen different directions, up into the surrounding trees. Wiggles quivered, and, honestly, so did I. It was quite a sight and honestly noisy. Their wings beating and their clucking make quite a racket.

Wiggles stayed put, and I stayed in the saddle, thank goodness. But Wiggles was a *shakin'* all over!

Things burst here at the ranch. Hope your world can avoid a burst or two!

TTFN,
Mia

A Love Story

Howdy, all:

Last week, Carry, the momma horse, suffered a bout of colic. That is a horse-sized stomachache that can be very serious. If colic is caught early, walking, oral pain medications, and water can avert a potentially life-threatening situation.

Carry was walked, given some pain medications, and I was holding her near the water trough awaiting the arrival of the vet. Prince came quietly over to Carry. And he softly whinnied and then gently started caressing Carry's stomach. Carry stood quietly while Prince nuzzled about on her ever so softly.

The vet arrived. Thankfully, the colic was mild, and Carry felt better as the pain medication took effect.

But Prince hovered around her for most of the afternoon.

And that is love, ranch style. Hope your world has a touch of love in it too.

TTFN,
Mia

Comings and Goings

Howdy, all:

Critters seem to come and go in unique manners. For example, the other morning, just outside my bedroom window was a *penguin*. I did not know that Texas had penguins! Well, sitting with his white chest puffed out and his black-beaked head was this *penguin* that was actually a very large hawk that had just had a meal of a blackbird. Feathers from the blackbird were scattered about, evidence of the event.

Doris the Deer came into the yard with Dorothy the Deer by doing the "deer limbo." She splayed her front legs and crawled under the electric fence while Dorothy leaped gracefully over. I watched Doris do this maneuver twice. She walked and trotted without a limp, so an obvious injury cannot be the reason she crawled rather than jumped the fence.

And now, the turkeys, the male turkeys, are in full regalia strutting through the yard with their harem. They cluck and click as they strut.

Finally, the three ponds now have been stocked with fish—bass, catfish, and hybrid striped fish.

The ranch has a lot of comings and goings each day. May your world be filled with likewise actions.

TTFN,
Mia

Facts about Longhorns

Howdy, all:

There are some facts that have been learned about longhorn cattle. Things that one would not even think of really.

Clara, the brown-and-white longhorn, and Willie, the black-and-white longhorn, are back on the ranch. They had been absent for some time. Clara had been on another pasture and had eaten some plant that caused her to develop a rash and then a sunburn. Did you know that longhorns get sunburned?

Something new under the sun for me.

And Willie has a slight limp to her left leg. She has arthritis. Even longhorns cannot dodge that malady.

Watching these two ol' gals is really a treat. They are grand beasts and seem to be very aware of the other. They scratch each other delicately with their very long horns. Quite something to watch.

Maladies strike even some of the ranch critters. So in your world, acceptance of what is is probably a good plan.

TTFN,
Mia

Luck of the Irish

Howdy, all:

This past St. Patrick's Day, Prince continued St. Patrick's tradition of kicking the snakes out of Texas (not Ireland). This remarkable event was witnessed.

Okay, the Brown Sisters Carry and Wiggles, the two goofy horses, were grazing near some small shrubbery. Prince was napping. All of a sudden, I saw him stride rapidly over to where the Brown Sisters were and saw him jab and strike and paw and then move quickly toward the brush pile. He continued to paw and snort and switch his tail and smack his lips even as I approached him. Then I looked where he was pawing. And the remains of a rattlesnake were there. He would not quit pawing until I had moved both Carry and Wiggles away. Then, he followed behind.

Whatta guy! Prince for prez! I checked all three horses for any sign of any bite from the snake, but thank goodness, there were none.

The Irish luck held here at the ranch. May a shamrock or two come your way.

TTFN,
Mia

49

Cat and Horse and Horse and Hog

Howdy, all:

Last evening, Peekaboo went out to investigate the shade tree where the vehicles park. Well, Wiggles saw Peekaboo at the base of the tree, and she, being Wiggles, headed over to check Peekaboo out.

Peekaboo saw her coming and scampered up into the tree.

Wiggles was not to be daunted. She stuck her nose up in the tree but could not reach Peekaboo. So she turned her behind to the tree and started *scratching* her behind on the tree, shaking the tree. Poor Peekaboo! He could not believe he was stuck in a shaking tree with a bratty horse causing the shaking!

Then, this morning, after a morning ride, the horses noticed that a half-blond, half-black little wild hog had come into the yard. Well, no hog gets in their yard, and all three horses with Prince in the lead took off after "Honeybear." That little hog ran off across the coastal pasture with the horses flying after it. He ducked into the woods across the fence. The horses took up a position of a guard under a small tree near the spot where the hog had disappeared.

Shakin' and runnin' here at the ranch. May your world have a bit of excitement.

TTFN,
Mia

Go Shovel Sand or Carry's Beach

Howdy, all:

Well, dear Carry, the momma horse, developed founder in her two front feet. Founder in horses can be, and is, serious. "No hoof, no horse" is the saying.

So after a stay at the horse hospital, Carry is home in a small pen filled with sand. The sand is soft on her feet while the healing continues. She has her own beach. She will be there another ten days and then will be reevaluated to see if she is sound for riding. Cross your fingers or cross your hooves!

In the meantime, preparations are being made for a big rain event due to start this weekend. Should be interesting. And a hog trap has been set near the Big Muddy. Honeybear, the half-blond, halfblack hog, met his fate from a neighbor. He is now in hog heaven. (Couldn't resist!)

Here at the ranch, we have our own version of a beach. May you have a sandy retreat in your world.

TTFN,
Mia

An Update

Howdy, all:

Well, Carry, the momma horse, appears to be much better. She has even slimmed down some. The Horse Weight Watchers' program has worked!

Jeremiah, the Muscovy duck that was living down by the bridge, has left. In her place is a pair of wood ducks. They are very skittish but so very beautiful.

At the Big Muddy, a trio of blue-winged teal is visiting. The male duck has an identifying crescent moon on his face.

Doris the Deer peeked at the yard the other morning and saw that the truck's hood was open with the battery charger attached. She was probably wondering when the rednecks had moved in!

Phidippides and Penelope, the caracara birds, have returned and are frequently seen gracefully soaring over the pasture.

And finally, Stumpy the Wild Hog has eluded capture. He has made his home somewhere in the brush on the slope, heading toward the creek. He is the ultimate *wild thing*.

A lot going on here at the ranch. May your world be a busy place too.

TTFN,
Mia

Petite Pepe le Peu and Peekaboo"

Howdy, all:

Peekaboo, the hunting cat, met Petite Pepe le Peu. It was an exciting meeting. And Peekaboo left the meeting "smelling like sweet roses." No, not really. He earned a bath after this encounter.

Phoenix, the other cat, looked so bewildered that a *skunk* was now in her house that in her very own rolly-polly fashion, she waddled swiftly to the highest point in the living room and kept a watchful eye for the *invader.*

Update on Carry. Yesterday, she went back to the horse hospital and got her follow-up hoof x-rays. All looks good for the ol' gal. And she celebrated coming home by literally "jumping out of the horse trailer" with joy. She and Wiggles and Prince frolicked and took off for the nearest patch of green grass. No more sand beach for her!

Smelling like roses here at the ranch. Perhaps your world has a pleasant scent to it also.

TTFN,
Mia

The Ups and Downs of Ranch Life

Howdy, all:

These past two weeks have been filled with events. Family came in for the Memorial Day Holiday. And along with that *up* came the *down* of Carry, the momma horse, getting so very ill after her bout and recovery from being foundered. She developed colitis with a fever.

So in the midst of all the excitement and activity of company, off to the horse hospital went Carry once again. Finally today after IV fluids, medications, antibiotics, and a lot of TLC, she seems to be on the road to recovery. May the alleluias ring out and bells peal with joy.

In the meantime, just as I was finishing mowing today, the ol' John Deer lawnmower "gave up the ghost" just at the crest of the hill. It is deader than a doornail. The good news is that I had just finished mowing.

The *ups* and *downs* of ranch life keep it from being stale. May no staleness be in your world.

TTFN,
Mia

The Prodigal Horse

Howdy, all:

Momma Carry horse is home, recovering from her horse-sized stomachache. She has her own pasture for she must remain isolated from the other horses until fully cleared of the "bug" that caused her stomach infection.

So Prince and Wiggles are outside Carry's pasture. They can see her, whinny to her, and be fairly close to her. They just can't physically contact her. And Carry gets special food throughout the day. Prince and Wiggles get a few treats here and there.

Now, what do you think Wiggles has done with all this attention given to her momma? She has run off! Just like the Aztec god, Quetzalcoatl. She has run to the front pasture, the Big Sandy, to be with her boyfriend, Svengali, the neighbor's horse.

Just like a teenager, she has run off and left her poor, ailing, heartbroken momma to recover all by herself. (Thankfully, stalwart Prince remains with Carry.) Hmm.

The horse world mimics us, or do we mimic them, here at the ranch. May your day be filled with a faithful steed.

TTFN,
Mia

52

Little Events

Howdy, all:

There are little events happening here at the ranch. Boots, the calf of Clara from two years ago, is expecting her first calf. We are all waiting for the arrival of her first babe. Clara's most recent calf, Bunny, was born on Easter Sunday. Clara and Willie are the ol' gals of the herd. They continue to grace the pastures with their long horns (no pun intended!).

Early this morning, Wiggles and I came across a fawn hiding in the brush. What a sight to see this delicate creature looking up at you with beseeching eyes.

Later in this morning's ride, we scared up a very small coyote. Let's hope Wily E. Coyote does not meet Bambi.

Carry continues with her recovery in her isolation pasture. Prince does lean over the gate each morning, checks on his gal, and then admonishes silly Wiggles as she tries to get his attention.

Little happenings here at the ranch fill the day. May fun adventures fill your world.

TTFN,
Mia

The Decision and the Three Wise Men

Howdy, all:

Recently, there had been serious chatter about closing the ranch down and moving onto a new chapter. But just like the *War and Peace* novel, there will be more chapters written at the ranch for the foreseeable future.

The latest chapter came last evening. Three *wise men* came to the feeding area. As the light was waning, three bucks showed up and munched on the feed in the backyard. What a sight to see. These three bucks were fairly young. They have earned the names Melchior, Caspar, and Balthazar.

And, on the Carry front, we now have two negative stools. Yeah. We need one more negative reading on her stool, and she will be freed from her isolation pasture. Cheer for negative poop!

The ranch has its own version of wise men visiting. May your world have some wise folks visiting.

TTFN,
Mia

Summer of Discontent or Life's Lessons through Horse Ownership

Howdy, all:

Here are some things learned from this summer of health challenges with the horses.

First, one will sweat if one owns horses. There is no mere glistening. Two, one's toes will get stepped on. So at the nail salon, be sure to get a nail polish that covers bruised toenails. Three, there is no such thing as a savings account. It is otherwise known as "Donations to your Local Veterinary Clinic Account." Four, you will need to learn to drive a truck with a horse trailer attached with a whinnying and anxious horse in the trailer. Five, you will need to move corral panels over and over and over again to form "isolation pens." Six, patience and more patience will be needed to figure out what the heck is going on with that big critter. Unlike Mr. Ed, they don't talk and tell you, "My tummy is hurting." And finally, one's wardrobe will consist of work shirts and jeans and a hat and a cooling rag. Forget any Vogue look!

So Carry had her third negative poop. She has been released from her isolation pasture, and she is doing well. Yeah. But Wiggles is now in the vet hospital with gunky drainage from her nostrils and high fevers. Lord, will it ever end?

Lessons learned on the ranch come in one thousand-pound packages. Hope your lessons don't weigh so much!

TTFN,
Mia

I See You, and I'm Home

Howdy, all:

The other day, while feeding the deer and rabbits along the creek, I came face-to-face with one of the most elusive creatures of the forest—a bobcat. He and I looked at each other in matched surprise, and then he gracefully and so very quietly slipped into a thorny hedge and disappeared. He was really no bigger than Phoenix, the feline Botticelli model cat.

And Wiggles is home from the horse hospital. She arrived home in a thunderstorm, just like the day she was born. Now, begins the three negative poop counts for her. Her horse-sized sinus infection morphed into a horse-sized stomachache, more than likely induced by the antibiotics she was on.

But she has slimmed down and is getting all sorts of attention. Being the attention queen that she is, she is enjoying her secondary gains as a patient!

Good events and wonderful sights at the ranch today. May your world yield likewise results.

TTFN,
Mia

Cowology

Howdy, all:

Recently, the ranch had some visitors, and a question about female longhorn cows was asked. So here is some *cowology.*

Clara and Willie are female longhorn cows, and they have long, long horns. Yup, female cows have horns in some breeds. Now, Clara, a brown-and-white cow, had a calf two years ago. That calf was brown-and-white at birth and is now black-and-white. That calf, Boots, has horns. But the horns are much shorter than her mom's horns. Boots just had her first calf. This calf is all black with a white face and has no horns. This new calf is named "Paleface."

This past Easter, Clara had another calf that also was brown-and-white. That calf has no horns and has remained brown-and-white. Her name is "Bunny." (Clever, no?)

So in the study of horns, cows, and colors, there probably are rules. Mother Nature and heredity are in charge. And that is probably where it should be left.

By the way, Stumpy, the wild hog, is now in "hog heaven," literally and figuratively speaking. Always learning here at the ranch. And may you pursue knowledge laced with wisdom.

TTFN,
Mia

Who or What Done It?

Howdy, all:

There is a mystery at the ranch—who or what put the remains of a skunk on top of the horse shed down in the horse pasture?

The other day, the last day Wiggles was in isolation, there was the fur and whatnot of a skunk on top of the tin shed. There are no trees close enough for a critter to climb up on the top of the shed; and being that the shed is tin, no creature could climb it.

Needless to say, Wiggles was all fidgety and ready to break out of her isolation pasture. Thank goodness she had been cleared by the vet that day.

All that remains is the mystery of how and what put the remains of a skunk on top of the shed. Hmm.

A head-scratcher at the ranch today. Pondering sometimes exercises the mind. Ponder away!

TTFN,
Mia

The Gaggle of Grackles

Howdy, all:

Well, in jolly ol' England, a crow is a sign of good luck. Here at the ranch, George and Georgette, the grackles, are a sign of good luck. (A tradition has started.)

What has been happening recently is that George and his mate have been showing up each morning with the ducks. George specifically carves out a "duck-free zone" for himself and then eats in peace. Georgette usually goes off and leaves him to it.

This grackle, with his less-than-harmonious song, hangs around most of the day. First in the backyard, then in the front. A *caw caw* here, a *caw caw* there; and as such amuses himself as he feasts on whatnot.

There is also a rumor that a panther has been recently spotted. These reports have been country legends for some time. As long as George and Georgette maintain their spot as resident alarm sounders, all is well here at the ranch.

Here at the ranch, any *caw* can be viewed as a good thing to have. Maybe in your world, something will serve as an alarm for you.

TTFN,
Mia

A Little Too Brave, Mr. Peekaboo

Howdy, all:

Ah, the proverbial morning in the backyard: coffee, sunshine, ducks, Phoenix, and Peekaboo. What could possibly go wrong? Hmm?

Well, into this idyllic scene came a bit of chaos. The ducks, with George the Grackle, were doing their usual feasting in the backyard. Suddenly, ducks and grackle were airborne, with the ducks hovering like squawking drones about eight feet above the ground. Onto the scene had come Mr. Wily E. Coyote. He was desperately trying to get some breakfast.

Mr. Peekaboo, seeing the invader in his backyard, puffed himself up to three times his size—almost as big as the Grinch's heart—and took off after the coyote. Oh, Lordy, Lordy, no, this is one critter you don't chase, Mr. Peekaboo! Coffee splattered, Phoenix rolled to another side, and one orange-and-white cat got scooped up before he and Mr. Coyote tangled. No need for that much bravery, Mr. Boo.

Thank goodness Mr. Coyote took off running, the ducks squawked and landed to finish their chattering meal, and Phoenix yawned and wondered what all the nonsense was about.

It's never dull at the ranch. May your world be lively too.

TTFN,

Another Mystery

Howdy, all:

Last week, before the welcome rains came, I did some shredding. Shredding is done by the big tractor with the seven-foot blade hooked behind the tractor. (In other words, mowing a big area—always in Texas!)

When I initially moved the tractor and shredder, scooting out from under the shredder was Pepe le Peu, the local area skunk. He was under there with a dead grackle bird. (Oh, no, Mr. and Mrs. Grackle!) Now, do skunks eat birds? I had no idea. Nearby, I found a pile of black feathers from what appears to have been quite a battle. Wha' happened?

So another mystery to be added to the life at the ranch.

Just in time for Thanksgiving, the turkeys showed up. There were twelve of them. Wonder if I should name them after the Apostles?

Mysteries at the ranch continue. May your world have a mystery or two.

TTFN,
Mia

Twelve Is a Good Number

Howdy, all:

On this first day of December, the number *twelve* has proven to be a good number.

First, there were twelve turkeys in the backyard this morning even with the sliver-colored coyote stalking them. The two "toms" of the turkey gang took off after Mr. Coyote. He was dispatched with their threats.

And then, the new herd of cows is twelve. Last week, they were turned out and promptly broke into two groups—one group of eight and one of four. Well, the group of four stayed right by the front gate and would not venture past Frog Pond. The group of eight was very adventuresome and traveled throughout the ranch. Just yesterday, the two groups met up, and now this morning, all twelve are together. They came by the house to get their dose of fresh water from the water trough.

A good dozen here at the ranch for the day. May your world have a good dozen too!

TTFN,
Mia

58

The Cow Race

Howdy, all:

Before the "Big Freeze" hit Texas, I was shredding the Big Sandy Pasture. And Blondie, one of the new cows, started running after the tractor, leading the entire herd of cows. They raced around the tractor and shedder. I had to slow down.

So here were the cows, all ten of them right behind Blondie with their tales high in the sky. "High tailin' it" for sure. They circled the tractor and then ran into the Tugly Woods.

Cows racing a tractor? Is something in the air? Did they get into the wacky weed?

A bit of nonsense here at the ranch. May your world have a bit of silliness in it. Enjoy.

TTFN,
Mia

The Twelve Turkeys of Christmas

Howdy, all:

The other day, I was on the golf cart doing chores. I was about to cross the bridge when I spotted the turkeys, the group of twelve, coming down the road toward me. I stopped short of the bridge and sat "stock-still."

Those turkeys came to a trottin' across the bridge, one by one, eyeing me with their turkey eyes. They would cock their heads to the side, cluck, do their turkey strut, and slowly and warily go by me.

It was the Christmas Turkey Parade by the Twelve Turkeys of Christmas.

'Tis the season of joy here at the ranch. May your holiday hold much happiness for you and all.

TTFN,
Mia

Wigglisms

Howdy, all:

Wiggles, the horse with more personality than Mr. Ed, has these endearing, sometimes-slightly irritating *isms*. For example, when I go to catch her, she always must check me out head to toe. She nuzzles my pockets for treats and then nuzzles all the way down to my boots.

When I put her halter on, she tosses her nose high in the air, as if to say, "Do we really need this thing?" Leading her to the hitching post to be saddled, she lets it be known that being ridden is "beneath her" (no pun intended). She hangs her head low, and I swear she *pouts*.

Riding her though is like an *E* ride. There is not a tree, a bush, a fluttering leaf, or a dove flying that she is not earnestly interested in. Her ears and eyes are always perked and sharply focused on her surroundings. She is not a "push-button" ride. In fact, have your seatbelt on and enjoy the adrenalin rush. But wherever you point her head, she will go. This li'l cow pony would have done well on the Pony Express. She knows one speed—fast—and she does it well.

Here at the ranch, we sit tight in our saddles. Hang on in your world!

TTFN,
Mia

Duckless Backyard

Howdy, all:

Where, oh, where have all the noisy, but loveable black-bellied whistling ducks gone? They are no longer coming to the backyard for their feeding sessions. The mystery continues as to what happened to them. They last appeared at Christmas and since then have been absent.

But in their place, there is a group of ducks enjoying the Big Muddy. They are black-and-white primarily and spring directly up from the water when startled. Unlike coots or mergansers, they do not *run* along the water before taking flight. And they are bigger than wood ducks. I have not yet been able to identify them. They are quite skittish and for good reason. Mr. Wily E. Coyote was stalking the banks of the Big Muddy the other morning.

Here at the ranch, there is some quiet to the mornings and afternoons. May your world have a touch of quiet.

TTFN,
Mia

Rodeo Time

Howdy, all:

The other day, the farrier came out to tend to the horses' hooves. And to make it easier for the farrier to get to them, they were in the small pasture. Without incident, their hooves were trimmed a "horse-sized" pedicure.

After the trim, the horses were let out of the pasture. Well, heck, you would have thought that they had been cooped up in small boxes their entire lives the way they came to a *runnin'* and *gallopin'* and *buckin*! Carry was especially joyful. She bucked, did a 360-degree spin, and bolted down to the Big Muddy with her tail a *flyin'*.

Wiggles did her best to keep up with the joyful antics of her momma. She reared up, bucked, and took off running after her mother. Dear Prince did his best show, but the girls stole the scene.

Pedicures bring such joy here at the ranch. May your world have such joy in the simple events.

TTFN,
Mia

A Discovery

Howdy, all:

Did you know that horses make good *watchdogs*, er, *watch horses*? Well, they do. Let me tell you about the watch horses.

The other day, Prince, Carry, and Wiggles were grazing in the coastal pasture. Idyllic morning, blue sky, birds chirping, you get the picture. Anyway, all of a sudden, and I mean all of a sudden, the three of them went into a full-startle mode. Heads up, ears pointed skyward, and snorting and galloping toward the house. It sounded and looked like the cavalry was a comin'. What in blazes had them all riled up?

Well, goodness sake, it was the troop of turkeys, with the two tom turkeys in full regalia, marching across the yard clucking away at the hens. The horses stood at attention while the turkeys marched single file through the yard toward the coastal pasture and finally into the woods.

Whatta sight. Horses announcing and saluting the turkey parade!

Visitors get announced here at the ranch. May your visitors be greeted warmly.

TTFN,
Mia

The Rescue

Howdy, all:

The other day, Wiggles and I took off for a ride. We started out along Miniature Pony Lane. Near the creek section of the fence line, we discovered a newborn calf (one of the neighbor's) curled up and caught in the leftover barbwire.

Wiggles was nervous about finding a calf caught in the wire. I took off her saddle and bridle and let her scoot back to the house—tail a *flyin'*. Then, I set about the task of getting the calf untangled.

It was surprising how strong the newborn was. It definitely had survival instinct in it as it fought me as if I were a lion of the jungle. But I was able to get it out of the wire and, miracle or miracles, no visible cuts were on it. The calf got up and, on its wobbly legs, started to run. I guided it back toward the neighbor's barn where the other cows were. A phone call to the neighbor completed the rescue.

Here at the ranch, we try to untangle things. Hopefully, in your life, you can untangle a few things too.

TTFN,
Mia

Lil' Stories

Howdy, all:

Have you ever seen a roadrunner "puffed up" sitting on the ground? The other day, there he was, Mr. Beep, sitting in the pasture puffed up to two to three times his original size. I simply don't know why. He then *unpuffed* and ran about his business.

Wiggles loves to roll in the mud, but gosh, she simply cannot get her delicate hooves wet when she is ridden. Oh, no, we must jump over the little puddle of water that is in the dry creek. Such a silly horse. However, she will go down to the Big Muddy and find the absolute muddiest spot and roll and roll and be so very proud of her "mud jacket."

Mr. Peekaboo has a lung infection and has been receiving daily medications for it. Well, he must be feeling better. He *attacked* Phoenix. He came out to the garage or otherwise known as the East Wing and promptly set about wrestling with that big, gray cat. Much to Phoenix's dismay, Mr. Boo is back!

Life here at the ranch in little stories. Your world probably has its own little stories.

TTFN,
Mia

Special Edition

Howdy, all:

Today, the eighteenth, is Wiggles's birthday. Yup, today, that li'l ball of fire came into the world.

But the story today is about her momma, Carry. I am thinking that Carry's name needs to be changed to "Mick Jagger" or "Lips." You see when you are giving the horses treats, Carry stretches her neck out as long as a giraffe's, and then, with her lips, she literally vacuums up as many of the treats as she can. And I mean even if one were a linebacker for the Dallas Cowboys, Carry could "knock you over" with her lips!

She is no fool. She usually places herself in the middle, between Prince and Wiggles, and thus gets a double helping of treats. The horses form a "treat line" as it were.

So to Wiggles's momma, today is a wonderful day. She gave birth just after the rain ceased, and Wiggles has delighted the ranch since that day.

Joy is celebrated at the ranch today. May you celebrate happiness in your world.

TTFN,
Mia

Phoenix the Mattress Cat

Howdy, all:

Phoenix is this adorable bundle of fur, a lot of furs, and well, fat. One could say she is the proverbial fat cat. When she is brushed, enough fur comes off that could stuff a mattress.

The other day, while brushing her on the front porch, the wind blew some of her furs off the porch, and it caught on the green grass blades. Early the next morning, a few enterprising birds, sparrow-like, were happily hopping about gathering up this fur for their nests. So indeed, her fur is being used for a mattress!

The ranch lurches into spring and early summer. The horses are fat, happy, and sassy on all the green grass. They are now, except for Prince, on a horse diet. "Lean cuisine" for the equine!

All are comfortable here at the ranch. May your world afford you some comfort.

TTFN,
Mia

Lazarus JD

Howdy, all:

It is one thing to deal with all the animals that are encountered on the ranch. It is entirely another to deal with the equipment on the ranch.

Okay, so the John Deere riding lawnmower has had many lives. It has been a mower, a *tugger*, a forest clearing machine. And its engine was getting weaker and weaker to the point that a blade of grass was causing it to falter.

So the local repairman put a new engine into the John Deere. Lazarus–like, the JD has arisen anew, complete with a new roar and a bit of smokin', just for added effect. The lawn gets mowed with ease. However, the new engine roar and occasional belch of smoke get every critter's attention.

No end to the variety of ranch living. May your life has variety too.

TTFN,
Mia

It's a Good Drink

Howdy, all:

Okay, my favorite drink during the day traversing about the ranch is an equal mix of diet ginger ale and cranberry juice. I have it in a nice tumbler.

This morning was no exception. I had my drink in the drink holder on the golf cart and headed up to get Wiggles for a morning ride. The horses were near Frog Pond, checking out the new cows on the neighbor's place.

I saddled Wiggles, took a ride, came across the momma turkey and her six *turkettes*. Had a wonderful ride and headed back to Prince, Carry, and the golf cart. Well, when I arrived back at the cart, I found Prince gulping the last drop from my tumbler. He was using the straw! He then smacked his lips and continued licking the tumbler and gave me a rumbling, well-contented whinny. I swear he was smiling. Funny critter!

The drinks are flowing here at the ranch. May you have many a refreshment in your world.

TTFN,
Mia

The Far Side Cows

Howdy, all:

You know, *The Far Side* was one of my favorite cartoons—ever. Just loved the cow cartoons, especially.

Here at the ranch, the cows personify those cartoons: Gigi, Bambi, Beauty, and her calf and the others. This morning, the cows were lined up along the road by Green Lips Pond. They really did not move even when I approached with the golf cart. Instead, Gigi turned to watch as I drove by. Don't you know that they got up on their hind legs as I went around the bend and commented on "that funny critter on that noisy thing!" (Think *The Far Side* cow comics!)

The turkeys continue to make their excursion to the backyard for their snacks. The cows watch the turkeys with their big beautiful cow eyes. One wonders what thoughts go through their brains as they stand, chewing their cud, watching these long-legged critters stroll by. Hmm. It would be interesting to find out.

Comedy is never far from the ranch. May your world have a little comic relief every now and then.

TTFN,
Mia

Deer Stomp Dance

Howdy, all:

There is a new dance step done here at the ranch. It is the deer stomp. Now, this all got started with Peekaboo thinking he is a cougar and the deer, Doris, his prey (or dance partner).

Peekaboo lies in wait for Doris. He flattens himself out, thinking his orange-and-white self is invisible on the green grass of the backyard. Doris comes in, and when the two of them lock eyes, the dance begins. Peekaboo's tail twitches ever so slightly. Doris stands and does her deer stomp dance—a little like a "cha-cha," stomp, stomp, stomp, rocker step, stomp, stomp, stomp, rocker step. And this goes on until the grand finale move by Mr. Boo (cougar in disguise). He leaps, pointing all paws and dashes at Doris. She does her classic spin and leaps up and over the nonelectric fence. Once over, she pirouettes and does some more of her stomp dance while Peekaboo goes back to his crouch waiting for another flying leap chance.

This dance can go on for a good cup of coffee and then some. Finally, Doris snorts and whisks her tail goodbye until next time. Peekaboo proudly prances back to the house, knowing that the dance was marvelous. (And the yard is safe from deer.)

Dancing 'til dawn here at the ranch. May your world have a bit of dance in it.

TTFN,
Mia

Cattle Rustling Twenty-First-Century Style

Howdy, all:

I am still free and not incarcerated for cattle rustling! (The next post may be from the local county jail, however.) And this is how it happened.

The neighbor, who runs cows out here, had gathered his herd to form a bigger group. The cows have to become a herd before turning them out onto a new pasture. All right, so for a few days, there were no cows on the ranch.

The next evening, while coming home, six rather wild-looking cows were munching in the Big Sandy Pasture. The neighbor called and asked, "Whose cows are those?" Heck if I know. How did I rustle these cows? They were not the neighbor's, so where did they come from?

Well, the fences were checked. A spot was found where the cows may have come through from the other neighbor's place. Maybe these *rustled* cows will find their way back to the proper pasture before the law catches up with me!

Trying to stay on the straight and narrow here at the ranch. May your path be the right path.

TTFN,
Mia

Life and Death on the Ranch

Howdy, all:

There is a poignancy about living out where the animals roam. One sees the circle of life occur. For example, yesterday morning, Mama Pepe le Peu tried to revive her youngster, seemingly with CPR-type efforts. It was in vain. The cause of death of the young skunk was undetermined, but Mama le Peu did not want to give up on her baby.

The lone female turkey, Amelia Turk, had a single turkette. She guards this li'l critter with all her vigor. She is very elusive and ducks into the brush at the slightest sound with her baby turkey. Hopefully, both will survive all that is out there.

And Carry, the dear momma horse, is struggling to recover from a serious case of the founder, lameness, brought on by sweet mesquite beans. Whether Carry can recover is unknown. Right now, she is in corrective "high heels" in her sand pen, and fingers are crossed that a tough decision does not have to be made.

The circle of life continues here at the ranch. And I bet the circle of life goes on in your world too.

TTFN,
Mia

Woohoo, I have Windows

Howdy, all:

The recovery of Carry continues. The vet came out yesterday, and according to the x-rays of her feet, there is healing occurring. She remains in her "high heels." They are on her front feet only and are glued on. (No kicking off those heels!)

Carry remains in her sand stall under the shed. But for the sake of breezes in this hot summer, a number of windows were cut out for her, and it was a bucking celebration on her part when she saw the windows in her shed. (She really did a buck or two and a small horse dance in her stall!)

Now, she leans out the window, Mr. Ed-like, and watches the comings and goings on the ranch. She can, with her loving eyes, watch you and get you to walk down with some juicy carrot treats for her. She just has her ways.

So continued healing for the ol' gal.

Here at the ranch, there are windows to see the happenings. May you have windows in your world.

TTFN,
Mia

The Ark Has Landed

Howdy, all:

Fins and flippers and oars and paddles have been put away. The *ark* has landed after the deluge here in Central Texas. All occupants here at the ranch are safe and sound.

Carry, Wiggles, and Prince took shelter in their shed. The windows were boarded up with plywood. The equipment trailer was moved into the garage, and the cats delighted in playing on it. The ducks took shelter behind the house from all the hurricane force-like winds and rains.

After the storm, Doris, Dorothy, and their two fawns showed up to eat their fill from the backyard feed line. Peekaboo kept a watchful eye on them, waiting for any dancing to occur.

Amelia Turk and her babe are safe in their home in the big oak tree in the coastal pasture. Thankfully, they weathered the storm also.

Winds and rains may blow, but all are safe at the ranch. May the tempest in your life bring no harm.

TTFN,
Mia

The Homely Cow

Howdy, all:

There is quite a herd of cows now on the ranch. Gigi and her calf, Beauty and her calf, Blackie and her calf, and quite a few others—some with names, some to be named.

But there is one cow that is so very homely. Poor cow. She is really quite, well, ugly. Yet, as homely as she is, one cannot help but adore her. Her name is Pig Pen. She has a face of a pig on a cow's body. Her legs are also quite short and stubby. She does get around though.

This morning, she was lollygagging in the creek, enjoying the mud and water seemingly unconcerned that she was making a mess. She simply got herself covered with mud and drenched with water, which made her ears sag even more.

On the Carry front, she continues with her convalescence. The high heels are still in place. Time and more "miracles" are needed to really heal her.

Looks don't matter here at the ranch. All are loveable. May the homely find love in your world.

TTFN,
Mia

Phoenix Rolls for Doris

Howdy, all:

Okay, Peekaboo is the "panther cat." Phoenix, on the other hand, is the "sleeping cat." Feline yin and yang.

This morning, Phoenix was napping on the back porch. Doris and Dorothy, the deer and their fawns, came into the backyard for their breakfast. Well, Doris saw Phoenix. Doris did her deer stomping and snorting at Phoenix. Doris then came to the very edge of the back porch. Phoenix, with owl wide eyes, looked toward Doris, wondering what all the fuss was about. What was this long-legged, snorting creature doing spoiling her nap? *What the heck?*, thought Phoenix.

So Phoenix rolled over and gazed back at me as if to ask what she was to do about her nap being so rudely interrupted. With that roll, Doris gave one last snort and stomp, flicked her white tail, gathered her group, and headed back into the woods. Phoenix blinked, yawned, and rolled back to continue her morning nap.

Good rest is taken seriously here at the ranch. May you get some rest in your world.

TTFN,
Mia

70

Cow Convention and Manure-ology

Howdy, all:

This morning, the first wave of the cowherd came up the hill, led by Gigi and Bambi, the two Brahma cows. Gigi is white; Bambi is fawn colored. Just like bookends, Gigi and Bambi stood on the backside of the Big Muddy, watching over the younger cows as they drank from the pond.

But later, Beauty, El Diablo, Cream Puff, Sparky, and the gang, Patch, Braille (a little calf born blind but has regained his vision), Big Red (the new bull), and Moonpie came up the hill a *hollerin'* and *bellowin'* for the others.

Gigi and Bambi and the others bellowed back, and a cow convention occurred just down the slope from the Big Muddy. All is well now that the herd has regathered. They lazily munch and nap the day away.

One thing cows make is, well, it is indelicate, but they make cow pies. And let me tell you something about manure-ology, hydrologists should study how effectively a cow pie can deter erosion. Cow manure on the gravel road is quite an impediment to erosion.

Here at the ranch, all things have their uses. May you find in your world the use for all things.

TTFN,
Mia

Comings and Goings

Howdy, all:

Here at the ranch, critters have their own way of *coming* and *going*.

Tall Pockets, the blue heron, glides gracefully in and lands without a splash on the Big Muddy. He is long and lean and so very graceful.

On the other end of the spectrum is the bumptious wanderings of Arnold the Armadillo. Arnold has made his home in the backyard and appears as evening light begins to show. What a display of amazing longevity for a critter. How has the armadillo made it all these years?

Anyway, he digs holes near plants. He may think he can dig to China. With these efforts, he is aerating the lawn, but only in the areas he thinks need it.

Here at the ranch, coming and going is part of the picture. May travels be part of your world.

TTFN,
Mia

The Vorpal Branch Went Snicker-Snack

Howdy, all:

The "Jabberwocky" came to life at the ranch last week. This is how it happened.

Wiggles and I started our ride heading around the Big Muddy. It was the day before winter was setting in on Central Texas. Sunny, clear, and quite warm ahead of a one-day cold front that had all creatures, large and small, scrapping for a good meal before tucking in for the cold.

Well, there was a noise heard coming from the edge of the Big Muddy, a muffled "Help me! Help me!" Wiggles snorted and stomped her feet. An investigation revealed a large green snake with a frog in its mouth. The frog was crying, "Help me! Help me!" At that point, the Jabberwock, with jaws that bite and claws—oh, wait, snakes don't have claws—okay, jaws that bite became the target for the "vorpal branch" that went "snicker-snack." With the very first blow of that mighty branch, the snake opened his jaws to holler, and out jumped the frog, hopping to safety as the Jabberwock was smitten by the vorpal branch.

No need to come *galumphing back* with the head of the snake. Hawk food was the order of the day for the slain snake. And thus, the sun shone, and the blue sky remained. Mr. Frog lives for another day.

Here at the ranch, those who ask for help will get it. May your cries be answered.

TTFN,
Mia

The Battle of Turkmyfoodistan

Howdy, all:

Okay, yesterday morning, an animal version of the Battle of Lepanto took place in the backyard. The players were Big Daddy Buck deer and the troika of turkeys.

Big Daddy Buck was eating his breakfast under one of the trees in the backyard. Soon after, the three turkeys, Amelia Airturk, her turkey, and Gimpy (the limping turkey), came into the yard. They started eating food under the other tree. Well, Big Daddy Buck finished the food under his tree and wandered over to join the turkeys.

That set off Amelia. She looked like a battering ram on legs. Her neck was stretched out long, and she charged the deer. (The sight of seeing a turkey launching herself at a buck was a coffee-spilling sight to behold.) Big Daddy Buck beat a hasty retreat to his tree, literally with his white tail tucked.

Amelia, satisfied that he was no longer a threat, waddled back to the other turkeys. And that, folks, was the battle of the "Turkmyfoodistan."

Food is quite vital here at the ranch. May your feast be uninterrupted in your world.

TTFN,
Mia

73

What the Heck Is This?

Howdy, all:

So last week, we were in the 80s. Then, we were not. And then, we had snow. Hmm.

Well, Prince, Carry, and Wiggles stuck their noses out of the shed, took a look around at the *white stuff*, and snorted. "What the heck is this?" They scampered out into the pasture and started pawing away at the snow to eat the green grass tucked under it. Then, they would scamper some more and paw again.

The snow covered and outlined everything in a fairly thick blanket. Animal tracks were visible in the backyard, indicating various visitors to the feed.

But the most shocked critter was Mr. Beep-Beep Roadrunner. He makes his home by Green Lips Pond. And he was standing roadrunner-leg deep, in snow, looking around as if to say, "Ma, I shouldn't have eaten so much last night. What the heck is this?" He literally just stood and looked about for a good while before he puffed himself up and took off a *runnin'*.

A surprise at the ranch is snow. May your world have a surprise or two for you.

TTFN,
Mia

Who Blinked First

Howdy, all:

Midmorning the other day, two groups of critters faced off. It went like this.

There were two groups of turkeys. The troika, Amelia's group, and a flock of twenty-four, many of which are toms.

Then, there was the herd of cows. Pig Pen, Beauty, Gigi, and fifteen others made up the current herd.

The big group of turkeys was in the backyard, feasting on the birdseed. They had finished and were clucking their way to the north lawn area. Well, the cowherd had come up, had their drink of water near the Well House, and now were heading back down the slope to the creek.

So on the north lawn were the turkeys. Just outside the electric fence on the north side of the house were the cows. The turkeys stretched their necks out and stared at the cowherd. The cow literally lined up single file along the electric fence and stared at the turkeys. This stare fest lasted for, well, some time. Now, who do you think blinked first?

Here's lookin' at ya at the ranch. May all you look at in your world be beautiful.

TTFN,
Mia

Glazed World

Howdy, all:

Well, freezing rain came yesterday morning to the ranch. Everything, even the clip on the gate to the horse pasture, was covered with an icy glaze.

Today, with the sun shining, the entire place looks like a crystal palace—a cold crystal palace for Central Texas.

The horses are full of vim and vigor and are enjoying munching on glazed grass in the coastal pasture. Meanwhile, the cats have figured out that heating pads are wonderful. Phoenix, the big gray cat, has her very own heating pad in the living room next to the coffee table. It is hers and hers alone. Peekaboo, the orange-and-white cat, has his on the back of the living room sofa. That is his perch so that he can survey his *kingdom*. Not that these cats are spoiled or anything!

There is ice on the water trough. A whack or two with an ax takes care of that along with the sun shining on it.

The ranch is all shiny with a gift from Mother Nature. May your world be as beautiful.

TTFN,
Mia

Bull and More Bull

Howdy, all:

The urban cowgirls were at it again. And this is how it happened.

Wiggles and I took off for a morning ride. She started fretting and acting so very antsy—more than normal. What the heck is up, Wiggles? Well, the next thing you know, we were face-to-face with a bull—the neighbor's bull—and voila, another younger bull—again, the neighbor's. Both had come out of the woods by the creek. Darn. Now what? Wiggles really did not like these intruders.

So upon investigation, Wiggles and I found the section of fence that the intruders came though. Okay, plan of action. How to get these two-ton critters back on their side?

Being an urban cowgirl, the ol' truck was employed rather than yeehawin' on Wiggles. Believe it or not, using the truck and the Oldsmobile car, both bulls were ushered through the broken fence back to their gals, and peace on Earth was reestablished.

We take no bull here at the ranch. May your world be "bull-free."

TTFN,
Mia

Prince and the New Put Put

Howdy, all:

Well, the often used and often, shall we say, abused golf cart died. It was a glorious death—complete with loud bangs and much clanking about.

A new golf cart has been secured, but, boy, Prince does not like it. He snorts and prances about, looking at it as if it is a fire-breathing dragon that has invaded his ranch. He arches his neck, points his ears skyward, and runs with tail *flyin'* whenever the new cart is used.

Now, Carry, on the other hand, comes over to the new cart, searching for treats. Prince stands warily back and *guards* her against the contraption. Wiggles a bit standoffish to the new cart also, but not quite as *riled up* as Prince.

The old golf cart will find its way to the usable parts store where nothing is wasted, nothing wanted.

Here at the ranch, a new thing or two comes in. May your world have a bit of new also.

TTFN,
Mia

The Audience

Howdy, all:

The other day, the veterinarian and the farrier came out to check on Carry's progress. She has li'l heels on. The farrier's father also came out. He is now semiretired from shoeing horses.

Carry was hooked to the hitching post near the garage. The farrier was working on her feet. Wiggles and Prince were behind her, watching the scene. At Carry's head, leaning on the hitching post, were the vet and the farrier's dad. Behind them, the cows were lined up in rows of two. First in line was Pig Pen and Beauty, then Gigi and Bambi, the Pirate and Sparky, and so on.

It was quite an audience for Carry's checkup. Of course, Carry was pretending not to notice all the attention, but you could tell she was soaking it all up.

The cows stood in rapt attention while the farrier and vet worked. They did not move until the farrier completed Carry's new set of *heels*. She is continuing to heal, thank goodness.

A star has been born here at the ranch. May your world have a new star also.

TTFN,
Mia

Cow Tales

Howdy, all:

Watching the cows gives one a lot of material for more *Far Side* comics. Those of you familiar with Gary Larsen's work will remember "Cow Poetry...Damn the electric fence! Damn the electric fence!"

Well, here are a few more tales to add. The neighbor's bull has become an adept visitor. He beats even the repaired fences. His name is, no joke, Houdini. Today, Houdini has joined the cowherd and lolls about with them as if he truly belonged. His owner is rigging up a supposedly *bull-proof* fence. Houdini is probably up to the challenge. (He has been observed jumping through the fence even leading a couple of his girlfriends to join him in his adventures.)

Pig Pen has her own version of *fencing*. She broke through the nonelectric fence (my bad) and was in the yard. She left her contribution to the greening of the world in the yard, not once but twice. And then she made her way over to the little garden by the garage, stood in the garden, looking into the garage, wondering why the golf cart was in there, and she was not.

Sparky and the gang, the young cows, kick up their heels and do high tailin', running anytime the pickup truck goes by. They might have a little *thoroughbred* horse in them!

The tales continue here at the ranch. May you have a few stories to tell also.

TTFN,
Mia

Cow Wash

Howdy, all:

Sparky and the gang were hanging around the car the other morning. Peekaboo, the cat, was out, and they were interested in this orange-and-white cat.

Peekaboo was making his early morning hunting rounds and had darted under the car when the cows approached.

The cows were trying to figure out where that cat had gone. Peekaboo cleverly snuck out from under the car and headed back into the garage. Meanwhile, Sparky and the gang were investigating all around the car.

When they could not find the cat, they began giving the car a *cow wash*, licking it as if it were a giant salt lick. They started on the windows and worked their way to the body of the car, not forgetting the rearview mirrors, which they adjusted in order to better see themselves. They finished their task and, like all good workers, headed for a ranch breakfast and fresh pond water.

Bring your car to the ranch for a good clean lickin'! May your world have a bit of silliness in it.

TTFN,
Mia

Rodeo Tryouts

Howdy, all:

The other morning, a crisp morning in Texas, the horses held their tryouts for the rodeo.

Prince was up first. He came out of the pasture with a twisting move and a front hoof jab, complete with a resounding snort. For good measure, he put a tail swish into the move.

Next up was Carry with her "high heels" flashing. She gave a long, stretched-out buck complete with a head shake and tail a *flyin'* behind her.

The final entrant was Wiggles. Oh, Lordy, she did a four-legged hop, straight into the air, with a solid four-legged landing, and straight into a rear-up with a loud snort and a dash to boot!

So who *won* the tryouts? Vote for your winner, and at the next rodeo, you can bet on your horse!

Having fun and frolic at the ranch. May you have some fun in your world.

TTFN,
Mia

A Horseshoe in the Hayfield

Howdy, all:

Perhaps all of you grew up thinking the saying was "a needle in the haystack." But you see, here on the ranch, it is a "horseshoe in the hayfield."

Now, Ms. Carry has been in "high heels," recovering and recovering well. These high heels are the equine version of Jimmy Choo's—a bit on the expensive side. The other day, the ol' gal decided she wanted to feel the grass. So she took off one of her heels. Lordy, Lordy, now where did she leave that heel or horseshoe? The farrier was called and wanted to know if the horseshoe could be found.

So the search was on. Wiggles was enlisted, and off through the pasture we went. Interesting things were found. A skull with canine-like teeth, feathers from a squabble, errant golf balls, but no horseshoe. Somewhere out there is that heel, and one day it may be found.

The farrier came out and gave Carry a new heel—keeps her balanced, you know. The search does continue, though, for the missing shoe.

Here at the ranch, the search continues. May your hunt be productive in your world.

TTFN,
Mia

A Lot Going On

Howdy, all:

It's been busy at the ranch: People are coming and going, and the critters have been busy too.

For example, Sparky, the young cow, decided he wanted the tractor and shredder out of *his* pasture. He chased the tractor, pulling the shredder until it was sufficiently out of his domain.

Then, we were riding Prince and Wiggles with Carry running wild and free. Carry decided to put on a cow roundup show. She dashed and pranced and put her tail high in the air and raced around the surprised cows, rounding them up in her very own "Carry fashion." She was in high spirits and was very much showing off to Prince and Wiggles.

And finally, in honor of Mother's Day, Pig Pen had her calf. Now, Pig Pen is a scruffy blond cow. Her calf is jet-black. His name is "JB," Jet Black. Yesterday, she whispered in the ear of Bandit, one of the young heifers, to watch JB while she grazed. Bandit stood right by the little newborn calf while Pig Pen went off and grazed to her heart's content. When she had had her fill, she came back, and JB got his meal.

Busy days at the ranch. May your days be filled with activities.

TTFN,
Mia

Cow Cart

Howdy, all:

Okay, at most ranches and ranchettes, it is called a golf cart. Not here at "Rancho Relaxo" as a family member calls it. It is called a *cow cart*. And here is why.

So a fence was needed to be checked. The cart was driven to the Big Sandy Pasture and parked in the shade. The fence was checked. And so back to the cart.

Surrounding the cart was the herd of cows, with Sparky, Beauty, Blondie, and Pig Pen being the ring leaders. All of them were innocently chewing their cud. The keys to the cart were gone, nowhere to be seen. The cart appeared to have been moved a bit, hmm…fishy? No? (Or cowy?)

Finally, the keys were found hidden in one of the cup holders. Now, how in the heck did they get there? No cow was admitting anything! Hmm. *The Far Side* continues at the ranch.

The ranch has a few innocent rascals. May your world have a few too!

TTFN,
Mia

The Bunny Hop

Howdy, all:

The other morning, Shadrach, Meshach, and Abednego, the three rabbits inhabiting the yard and close environs, were having a game of rabbit tag. They would race after one another, stop and catch their breath, and go again with the chase.

Mr. Peekaboo wanted to get in on this game. He went out to join, and the rabbits let him play. However, they incorporated a twist into the game. They instituted a hop—a straight-up jump with a kick of one's heels. Peekaboo got into it and did the *bunny hop.*

The game went on until the rabbits realized it was time to head to their daily hideaways. Perhaps in the evening, they could all play again.

Peekaboo had had such fun. He was disappointed when it ended, and if he had been a young boy, one could say his shoulders sagged as he sauntered slowly back into the house.

Here at the ranch, our days have a bit a hop to them. May your world have a little bounce too.

TTFN,
Mia

JB's Roundup

Howdy, all:

Jet Black, Pig Pen's calf, has a habit of straying solo from the herd. The other day, he was napping, and napping, and more napping down by the Big Muddy while the herd lumbered down the slope to the creek area.

When he woke up, he looked about, bleated out a plaintive *moo*, and trotted toward the feed shed and then the water bucket. No cows were around. So he trotted back to the Big Muddy and wandered around for some time, wondering where the herd had gone.

Dusk was rapidly approaching, and alone li'l calf is not safe out here on the ranch. A roundup ensued. Using a feed bucket, some imitation *moo, moo, mooing,* JB moved down the slope. He stopped halfway and would go no farther. Okay, then, off to find Pig Pen. She followed the feed bucket very readily, and, as she was looking for JB, she crossed the bridge and up the slope where a very happy reunion took place just as the sunset. Whew!

Sunsets do bring peace to the ranch. May the evening time be restful in your world.

TTFN,
Mia

Sightings

Howdy, all:

There have been some unusual sightings lately at the ranch. The first of these occurred midmorning. Along the section of the road that parallels the creek, there was a momma deer. I think it was Doris with three fawns. The fawns were spry but so very small. Two days in a row, they were seen. "Deer preschool," I believe it was.

The next sighting was Shadrach, one of the backyard rabbits, sitting between two tom turkeys. Can you imagine you are this small rabbit looking up at these long-legged critters complete with red *moustaches*? Would that not cause you to eat different foods?

And the final sighting was the newborn calf Blondie. Now, Blondie is this big, yes, blond cow with ears that catch the wind. She has a challenging face; that is, she lets you know she is the boss and not to mess with her. Her calf is a small bundle of blond legs and tail. He is a chip off the ol' rump, so to speak.

Lots to see out here at the ranch. Hope your world affords a lot to view.

TTFN,
Mia

Hey, Diddle, Diddle

Howdy, all:

Some of you more seasoned individuals will recognize the childhood ditty, "Hey, diddle, diddle, the cat and the fiddle, the cow jumped over the moon." Well, there is some truth to that rhyme.

There were three cows, all golden blond, from the neighbors. They decided to come for a visit. Tweedle-Dee, Tweedle-Do, and Tweedle-Dum, the trio, got themselves into a conundrum. (Cow Poetry, don't you know.) Anyway, they got here to visit, but how the heck were they to get back to their own group?

These three trotted at a good pace up and down the fence lines, mooing at any and all other animals as if asking directions to the nearest break in the fence to cross. After a considerable search, Tweedle-Dee took things by the horns and led the merry band of wandering cows to a low spot in the fence, and up and over the three went, leaping the *moon*.

All are in their place here at the ranch. May all be where they belong in your world.

TTFN,
Mia

Eatin' on the Run or Be New York

Howdy, all:

You know how it has been said of New Yorkers that they eat while walking down the streets of NYC. Well, here at the ranch, Wiggles "eats on the run" on her *street'* in the horse pasture. It goes like this.

The horses are in the small pasture by the shed to stay away from mesquite beans. These beans are what caused Carry to founder because of the high sugar content in them. So this small pasture is clear of any and all mesquite. The heat of the summer has dried up the grass in the pasture; thus, the horses are fed coastal hay. The hay is placed in a cool and shady area of the pasture.

As the hay is being walked down to that cool and shady corner, Wiggles trots along and grabs a big ol' bite of coastal and munches on it—New York style—down her path. She is not one to miss out on food—that is for sure! I think she would be right at home in the Big Apple because she loves attention. Broadway, watch out, here comes Wiggles!

Here at the ranch, we are munching our way through our days. Hope your world has a snack or two!

TTFN,
Mia

Roundup Cats

Howdy, all:

Last week, the skinny bobcat that makes her home near the creek revealed why she is now so skinny. Twiggy, the bobcat, has had babies. And she was on the bridge with two of them.

When Twiggy and her family were startled, of course, one kitten went off to the left of the bridge, and the other kitten went off to the right. Twiggy darted after the kitten that had veered to the right and scruffed him up by the neck and dashed back after the one that had gone to the left. Even cats have difficulty rounding up other cats!

So hopefully, the Twiggy family is doing okay even with the heat and the dry, very dry conditions of this Texas summer. Thankfully, the creek continues to run. It is the source of cool water for many.

All are trying to stay together here at the ranch. May your world have a good togetherness.

TTFN,
Mia

Rains Cometh

Howdy, all:

Well, the rains have come—thankfully. Each day for the past week, the ranch has received measurable rain. With this rain, the Big Muddy is filling up again. Maybe it will get full enough to cover the evidence of a stuck tractor near its center. (A long, hot, muddy story for some time later.)

With the softened soil, Arnold the Armadillo has been busy at work in the yard. Arnold likes to dig narrow trench-like holes throughout the yard. He also does a very good job of tilling the lawn in various places. He turns the sod over, looking for food, or he truly is helping aerate the lawn!

Even though the grass in the pastures has started to green back up, Sparky waits behind the feed shed each day, seeing if he will get a treat of some coastal hay.

The black-bellied whistling ducks have returned with their young brood. They really appreciate that the Big Muddy has some water back in it so they can float and whistle-quack at one another.

The ranch was blessed with rain. May your world receive a blessing.

TTFN,
Mia

Using Flowers as a Guide

Howdy, all:

So Henry the Hummingbird got himself into the garage the other day. He was not having any of the *direction* being given to him by the blue minnow net. And Henrietta, his mate, was buzzing around the house, wondering what the heck he was doing in the garage.

Plan A, the blue minnow net, did not work.

Time for plan B. Some beautiful purple flowers were gathered and tied to the emergency release string that hangs down from the opened garage door. Then, some plastic flowers were put on the floor near the purple flowers. Now it was a waiting game to see if plan B would work.

After about forty minutes, Henry got himself out of the garage, and Henrietta gladly met up with him. The two of them then raced around the house like miniature planes in an aerodrome race. They have a lot of flowers to tend to.

Getting outside is important here at the ranch. May you enjoy the great outdoors in your world.

TTFN,
Mia

A Ranch Version of Lac Qui Parle

Howdy, all:

There is a lake in Minnesota named "Lac Qui Parle," the lake that talks. Here at the ranch, there is a backyard that *talks*. The talkers are the black-bellied whistling ducks and the now ever-growing flock of turkeys.

The ducks fly in each morning and start their chatter. There are two distinct groups of ducks, and they quack and whistle at one another, fussing about who gets what food.

Then, the turkey gang trots in. And, boy, the gobbling and quacking really get going. "Might" makes the food mine; that is, the bigger the bird gets the pick of the food.

And that is how the backyard is the "yard that talks" or "Yarde Qui Parle."

The ranch has its talkers. May your world have the listeners.

TTFN,
Mia

Ma, Where's My Winter Coat?

Howdy, all:

The dramatic has always been associated with Texas. The weather is no exception. So one day, it is in the 90s: the next, it is in the 40s with cold rain.

Wiggles, Prince, and Carry all hurried into their shed with Wiggles snorting at Carry, her mom. "Mom," she seemed to be saying, "where is my winter coat?" You see, with the weather having been in the 90s for the weeks and months before, the horses' winter coats had not started to grow. So here they were, with summer coats and Mr. Winter setting in.

Now, no worries about these pampered critters. They were given cover and food and water and an extra treat or two. As the days progressed, the weather moderated, but the horses' instinct has them growing their winter coats.

Here at the ranch, preparing for winter is happening. May your preparations go as planned.

TTFN,
Mia

Et Tu, Gravel Pile

Howdy, all:

Last week, a pile of gravel was delivered to help repair soft spots in the road. The pile was placed near the Well House.

For some reason, the cows seem to love gravel piles. And Sparky seemed to take an especial interest in it. After pawing a bit at the pile, Sparky backed up, put his head down, and charged it. He did this a number of times, shaking his big head in the gravel after each collision. "Take that, gravel pile," said Sparky, or "Et tu, gravel pile."

After a few rounds with the pile, Sparky backed up one more time, gave a cow buck, put his tail high in the sky, and took off to join the other cows. He had done his duty and had tackled the gravel.

The gravel was put to its original use to help the road to the ranch. Sparky's pile is no more.

Things are often spread out here on the ranch. May items in your world also be likewise spread.

TTFN,
Mia

Warrior Horse

Howdy, all:

Sometime before Thanksgiving, a battle took place on the ranch. This battle was witnessed while gathering firewood for the coming winter months. It went like this.

Prince, Carry, and Wiggles were on the top of the slope, grazing peacefully in the coastal pasture. Down toward the creek, the *invaders* were crossing south to north, heading toward the wilderness pasture on the north side of the ranch. The invaders were wild hogs.

The minute Prince saw them, he flattened his ears, barred his teeth, and charged full tilt toward them. Boy, did he charge! He chased them across Poor Man's Pasture, through the coastal pasture, and into the wilderness pasture. Carry and Wiggles ran gaily behind him, thinking it was such fun to gallop about. But Prince was all business. He stood guard, snorting and pawing, where the hogs had disappeared. He stood there for most of the afternoon.

Charge of the Warrior Horse. Beware, wild hogs, he is on guard.

The ranch has its own guardian. May your world also have a guardian.

TTFN,
Mia

New Tactic for the Deer Hunt

Howdy, all:

Well, Mr. Peekaboo, the deer-hunting cat, has come up with a new tactic to *bag* himself a deer. You see, the deer have been frequenting the backyard feed line. Mr. Boo has been waiting for them by the backdoor. He then slowly but surely does his crouch approach, thinking that his orange-and-white self is invisible against the green grass. Now using this technique, he has gotten quite close. But the deer are able to elude him.

Time for a new approach. Yesterday, Doris and her three fawns were munching in the backyard. Peekaboo went around through the open garage door and thought to sneak up on them from a new angle. He crouched, inched forward, crouched, and inched forward; and just when it seemed he had one of the fawns in his sights, Doris snorted and stomped, and off to the woods the deer went.

Darn, he thought, *this new approach didn't work either.* Peekaboo trotted back to salve his feelings and jumped into the bed of the truck to wait for the next chance at venison.

The hunt continues here at the ranch. May your search continue in your world.

TTFN,
Mia

The Golf Ball Mystery

Howdy, all:

Some folks came out and were hitting golf balls into the backyard and toward the Big Muddy. So the next day, the hunt for all the golf balls commenced. All were found and picked up from the backyard for sure. Those in the Big Muddy are lost until the next drought dries up that pond.

Two days later, a golf ball was found literally in the middle of the backyard, right smack in plain view. How did it get there? Where did that doggone golf ball come from? A mystery for sure.

Along with that mystery, Peekaboo is now waiting for the deer at the base of one of the trees in the backyard. The deer are *playing along* with this new game of "hunt the deer by the cat." So funny!

A mystery at the ranch adds a bit of spice to life out here. May your world have some spice to it.

TTFN,
Mia

Bovine Bulldozers and Tree Trimmers

Howdy, all:

Down by the Big Muddy, there is a Memorial Garden, with decorative plants, trees, and shrubs. Each one symbolizes a deceased family member. The garden is surrounded by a split rail fence that has personality. It has certain leanings if you catch the drift.

With all the recent rains, the fence posts have developed more *leanings*. And the cows, especially Blondie and Pig Pen, have decided to employ themselves as bovine bulldozers and take down the fence. After they had knocked down part of it, they were hungry. They did further work by trimming all the plants, trees, and shrubs. Hmm. Thoughts of hamburgers and steaks came to mind after seeing what those bovine contractors had done.

So if you are in need of some bulldozing, some trimming, they are ready to assist you. Just dial 1-800-IAMASTEAK.

It is never dull here at the ranch. May your world be also filled.

TTF,
Mia

Chores and Rewards

Howdy, all:

This morning's chores included taking care of feeding the yawning maw of Phoenix, the "Garfield" cat of the ranch, tending to laundry, and gathering the trash to take to the end of the lane.

While emptying the last of the trash cans in the garage, a *reward* was sighted. Doris, the deer, and her three youngsters were having deer games in the horse pasture. (I guess deer and reindeer play games.) They were dashing about playing tag, ring around the tree, and "see how high I can jump." Whitetails were flashing high and straight as they competed in these games.

This wonderful sight lasted for some time until Doris decided it was enough, and off into the woods they all trotted.

Work has its rewards here at the ranch. May your chores be rewarded.

TTFN,
Mia

And They Marched One by One

Howdy, all:

The black-bellied whistling ducks have a new approach to the feed line in the backyard. It goes like this.

They circle in the air a couple of times over the backyard, whistling and checking out the scene below to make sure all is clear. Then, they land in the clearing just beyond the backyard's electric fence line.

There they sit and congregate and have a good ol' meeting, fussing at one another and, in general, chattering up a storm.

After a bit, this meeting comes to a close, silence ensues, and one duck takes the lead. He points his beak at the feed line and begins the march, in true duck-walk fashion. The other ducks line up behind him, one by one, and march in step with him to the feed.

The feasting begins. A whole new chatter storm starts up as they squabble over the food. If another group of ducks comes, they duplicate this approach, and boy, oh, boy, does the duck chatter increase in volume!

Here at the ranch, the line forms in the yard. May the line not be long in your world.

TTFN,
Mia

The Bad Example of Pig Pen, the Escape Artist

Howdy, all:

Pig Pen is an escape artist. She can climb like Sir Edmund Hillary; she can wiggle out like Houdini. She is a cow making her own path.

Now, it is one thing for Pig Pen to partake in these capers. But she has been a bad example to the other cows, especially Blondie. Blondie took the example of Pig Pen and climbed down into the creek, waded across it, and scrambled up the other bank into the racehorse pasture. The grass is really greener on the other side of the creek.

Blondie did this last week. She was rounded up and put back with the group. But today, she did it again; so this time, she will be moved from the ranch. Darn. Why, Blondie, why?

We try to keep the grass green here at the ranch. May your world stay green also.

TTFN,
Mia

88

The Ducks of March

Howdy, all:

So, the "ides of March" may have been more of a historical event than the "ducks of March" on the ranch. But then again, that was Rome; this is Texas.

The ducks are really quite clever critters. The other day, they circled about, doing extra loops over the feeding area in the backyard until the deer had left. They then landed in the pasture and. did their march one by one into the yard to the feed line.

Today, the ducks ate their fill and left for the Big Muddy. They sat at the edge of the Big Muddy until they saw that more feed had been put out. Can you believe they came back for round two of breakfast? They are no fools—no bird *brains* here!

The ranch always has more food for all. May your world feed you well.

TTFN,
Mia

A Roman Aqueduct Comes to the Ranch

Howdy, all:

The Romans of old had their aqueducts. And the ranch will have a buried water pipeline, shipping water south to the San Antonio area. Big trucks, bulldozers, and other heavy equipment are moving to and fro, busy as bees getting this pipe laid and buried across the narrow neck of the road near Slide Corner. Slide Comer is the big corner of the road just under the power line. The pipe follows the power line path.

All of this construction and activity has the critters both nervous and curious. The horses watch the activity yet snort and prance when it becomes too much for their curiosity. What this activity has caused is for Pig Pen's newborn calf, a jet-black calf (hence named Jet), to crawl under the fence and hide in the Tugly Wood.

So Pig Pen had to be reunited with her calf. She was rounded up and moved to that side of the fence. They are now very happy to be back together again.

Togetherness is valued here at the ranch. May you be with those you love.

TTFN,
Mia

A New Deere at the Ranch

Howdy, all:

Well, the ol' John Deere gave its last gasp mowing around Carry's pen. She had an abscess on her right foot and needed wet-to-dry dressings applied to that foot to drain the abscess. Her pen needed a li'l trimming. The John Deere mower huffed and puffed through this task and, then, in a final wheeze, had a glorious BANG backfire. A fitting end to this marvelous machine.

It had mowed paths in the woods, plowed through knee-high grass in the pastures, trimmed the grass along the lane, and. mowed the yard around the house. This mower did things not meant for lawnmowers to do. But those tales will never be totally revealed. They could prove to be embarrassing.

So off to the John Deere shop and a brand-new, shiny Deere graces the garage. The critters have reluctantly accepted this new machine.

Here at the ranch, we have brought in the new. May your world have something new too.

TTFN,
Mia

Rabbit Tales

Howdy, all:

It has been written that the reason rabbits are associated with the Easter season is because of their long legs. The tale goes as follows. When rabbits are being pursued, they are their fastest when running uphill toward heaven. Thus, rabbits are linked to the "rising to heaven" of Easter time.

Here at the ranch, the rabbits are in full swing. Last evening down near the horse pasture, there was a trio playing rabbit tag. They were playing inside the stacked-up panels. The panels form a triangle. That makes an area perfect for the rabbits to play in.

The horses leaned over the panels to watch as these darting rabbits had their fun. What the horses did not realize is that some carrots were tossed into the triangle for the rabbits. Hmm.

Runnin' fast comes in handy at the ranch. May speed help you in your world.

TTFN,
Mia

A Bittersweet Beginning

Howdy, all:

A certain lanky character has been hanging around the ranch for the past five years. He and his sister first visited the ranch many years ago when this operation was just in its infancy.

He has endured mud from the Big Muddy, traps for hogs, and poison ivy while clearing fence lines. He has built many interesting items, one of which is a homemade bow from a plastic pipe. He has cut wood, chopped down cactus plants, trimmed trees, and has had certain experiences with the golf cart.

Now this lanky Texan is off to drive tanks for the army. It is a bittersweet beginning for this young man as he leaves the ranch to tackle his profession. All the critters, from Pig Pen to Wiggles to the "phat cat," Phoenix, wish him all the best. He will be missed. Soldier on, dear Emory.

The ranch is still and quiet. May your world have peace.

TTFN,
Mia

The Travails of Jet

Howdy, all:

Okay, Jet is Pig Pen's calf. He is jet-black. Jet is the only bovine that comes into the yard. He has figured out how to squeeze under or between the wires of the electric fence. It probably would help if the electric fence were turned on, but sometimes, it is a task forgotten. He has also figured out how to sneak into the horse pasture and graze all by his lonesome.

But today, Jet got himself in hot water with Pig Pen. They got separated. The wailing and mooing were biblical. Pig Pen mooed; Jet let out a plaintive wail. When they finally found each other, Pig Pen let out one final *moo*, telling Jet that he was never to cross the pasture again without letting her know.

Later in the morning, Pig Pen had Jet right by her side, not letting him romp with Cream Puff his buddy. It appears he is *grounded*. The question is, How long will he behave?

Order and peace have been reestablished here at the ranch. May there be peace in your world.

TTFN,
Mia

The Help, Bovine Style

Howdy, all:

"It was a dark and stormy night," wrote Snoopy. And since it is Texas and the ranch, let's throw in some hellfire and brimstone for good measure. It was a storm that blew through here the other night. The howling winds brought down a few branches here and there. A couple of the downed branches were by the bridge. Those branches really needed to be moved.

The cows decided to pitch in and help, especially Gigi and BNW. (She is black-and-white.) Gigi led the cleanup *moo-crew*. She and her cohorts started to munch their way through the branches, making them lighter and easier to move. Fleabite and Beauty also decided to *lean in* and give some help. They used some of the bigger branches as scratching posts. That moved the branches too.

Just a little bit of work by the chainsaw finished the job after the Bovine Crew had done their part. The road was clear again for all.

Here at the ranch, we use all the *mooscles* we can get. (Couldn't resist!) May you have the strength you need in your world.

TTFN,
Mia

Pig Pen Living the High Life

Howdy, all:

Pig Pen and her calf, Jet, have had a few adventures recently, living the high life here at the ranch.

Their first escapade was to throw a *pond party* for all the cows, or at least those who dared to get more than their hooves muddy. With all the rain recently, there is a new *pond* in the woods near the bridge. It is shaded and cool and oh, so muddy. What a splashing success the pond party was!

Next, they thought it fitting to have some tea on the front porch of the house. Why not? Sensing that the electric fence around the house was off, into the yard came Pig Pen and Jet. Jet got on the front porch and was checking out the rocking chairs to see which one was the best fit. Hmm.

The final adventure was the one that got Pig Pen and her band of followers into a bit of trouble. She led a crew of four cows into the neighbor's pasture. She had found a small opening in the fence that was caused by the recent flood.

Well, now, Pig Pen, Jet, Blondie, Jet Black, and Beauty are in a penitential pasture by their cowboy owner.

Some adventures can lead to trouble here at the ranch. May your adventures be trouble-free.

TTFN,
Mia

Phoenix Takes Up Housework

Howdy, all:

The ranch has two cats: one gray and one orange-and-white. The gray cat, Phoenix, in all her splendor, has a PhD in lounging. She has perfected the technique of a nap to a *T*.

Once in a great while, she will stir. Not at any rapid pace, mind you. She delights in lolling about and moving at a sedate speed. No hurry in this gal!

The other day, however, she wanted to join in on the housework. The cabinet where the Windex and other supplies are kept was open. Into the cabinet went Phoenix, seeking to assist in the cleaning tasks. After a very short while, Ms. Phoenix decided that her forte was not housework. Instead, she waddled over to the refrigerator and promptly settled down right in front of it. Now that means only one thing. The work is done. Food is to be served and on a napkin, please.

Thus, ends the foray into housework for Phoenix. Back to designing new napping styles. Much better work if you can get it.

The housework at the ranch can be a team effort. In your world, may all pull their fair share of chores.

TTFN,
Mia

News Flash—Hot in Texas in July

Howdy, all:

It may come as something of a surprise, but it is hot in Texas in July. Yup, the critters know to stay low during the heat of the day. In fact, the horses and cows have a favorite spot down by the creek in the shade. They congregate there for the afternoon siesta. Each of them vies for the prime spot in the shade and on the cooler soil for their nap.

As evenings approach, horses, cows, deer, turkeys, ducks, and all other assorted creatures begin to move and graze and wander through the pastures on the ranch.

The ponds are holding their own as the bountiful spring rains helped to fill them. Here is hoping they hold until the next rain comes, which, at this point, is not in the near future.

Last week, we had a few days of "cooler weather." Carry led a dash up the hill with her tail a *flyin'* to celebrate. She even threw in a few equine pirouettes for good measure.

Shady areas are sought here at the ranch. May you find a cool spot in your world.

TTFN,
Mia

Mr. Longneck Comes for Breakfast

Howdy, all:

Early in the mornings, Mr. Longneck (that is, big, daddy turkey) comes for breakfast. He struts in and shoos the chattering ducks aside so that he can eat his fill.

This morning, Ms. Phoenix decided to trundle to the back porch for her morning nap. In all her glorious grayness, she lumbered through the partially propped open backdoor. (She had to nudge it a bit to fit through!) She made her way onto the porch and became visible to Mr. Longneck. Well, that started the long neck to get stretched and more stretched to check out what that gray matter was. He stared a very long time, making sure no threat was coming his way. Little does he know that there is no threat from Phoenix. She only *threatens* her food dish!

After a very pregnant pause, Mr. Longneck went back to eating breakfast. He got his fill and then turkey-trotted on to find his mates. There are about eleven young turkeys. He is a busy man.

The morning meal is important here at the ranch. May you enjoy your first meal of the day.

TTFN,
Mia

Unicorn or...?

Howdy, all:

The other day, it was noticed that Wiggles had a bony prominence between her ears. Does that mean she is a fledgling unicorn?

It would appear Wiggles thinks of herself as more than a horse. You see, she takes her feed bucket and flips it over after gobbling up her daily dose of feed. Then, she heads over to Carry's bucket and tries to snag some of her food. If that doesn't work, she very carefully inches her way toward Prince's bucket and, with her lips, tries to move the bucket out from under him. Prince, of course, does not stand for this theft.

Wiggles then leans over the gate and, with those big, brown eyes, tries to coax more treats her way. She is a good beggar—a very good beggar. Her looks of absolute desperation for food are almost convincing.

But wait, upon closer inspection, there are two bony projections between her ears. Does this mean she is a—? Aha, the mystery!

The mischief-maker has a place here at the ranch. May your world allow for a bit of mischief too.

TTFN,
Mia

Manure-ology

Howdy, all:

When the Romans were building the Appian Way, they probably used what materials were available to them. Here at the ranch, the same concept applies.

Earlier in a discussion, it was mentioned that cow manure helps prevent erosion. The gravel road here at the ranch is prone to being washed away in the heavy rains that occasionally come through. So manure is put on the road to try and reduce this erosion.

Now, think about it. Manure is readily available. (Boy, howdy, is it ever!) It is biodegradable. It is heavy, no joke there. And it does provide a cushion once it dries to the sharp edges of the gravel. The hope is that not only does it help with reducing erosion but that it will also form a biomass that will encourage some vegetation to grow. That vegetation may also help reduce the washing away of the gravel. We can hope.

It may not be a Roman road here at the ranch, but it is passable. May the roads in your world be in good shape.

TTFN,
Mia

Spike's Gang

Howdy, all:

Here at the ranch, Spike, the young buck deer with one antler, is leading a *gang* of deer. He has approximately seven deer in his group. Doris and her new young one, Dorothy and her twin fawn, and a few more make up the group.

Each day, they await the *put* sound of the golf cart heading up the lane. That sound means food, deer corn. They hide along the road near the creek bed. When the golf cart passes by, they know that corn is being tossed out in large handfuls. They eagerly gobble it up.

Some of the fawns still have their spots. They give due deference to the older deer for the food. Otherwise, if they don't behave, Doris or Dorothy or Spike enforces *table manners* with a quick thrust of a leg or two. When they have all finished, they dart back into the woods.

The gang is happy, fat, and sassy here at the ranch. May your group be happy also.

TTFN,
Mia

Mother Nature's Curlers

Howdy, all:

The rains have been sparse this summer and early fall. The grasses have turned from the rich, spring green to a dusty, dry brown. The cows munch on leaves and shrubs. And then as a beloved sister called them, Mother Nature's Curlers, a big, round bale appears.

When these bales are placed in the pasture, usually in the Big Sandy, the cows gather around them (no pun intended) like guests at the feast table. All one sees are happy cow behinds and their tales occasionally flicking at pesky flies.

The bales take on unusual shapes as they are consumed. At first, yup, they are round. Then, some develop giant tunnels in them. Other bales are formed into wedding cake designs, with a tall center cone remaining and crumbs about.

Once in a great while, the horses will deign themselves to have a nibble or two; but you see, those bales are *cow quality*, not quite up the standards of the equine world. Oh, the spoiled equine world of the ranch.

The munching continues here at the ranch. May you have a good snack or two in your world.

TTFN,
Mia

A Dash for Cover

Howdy, all:

The fall season has arrived, and with it is a blast of cold rain (much-needed rain). The storm came in the other evening with the winds switching from south to north and the dark clouds racing across the sky.

The horses had just finished their evening meal and were casually heading down the hill toward the creek when this storm was approaching. In a matter of minutes, the warmth gave way to cool and then downright cold rain. Carry, Wiggles, and Prince backed their behinds to the forest, which blocked most of the north wind. There was lightning, and in this strobe-like atmosphere, their eyes shone turquoise bright whenever a flash occurred.

A loud whistle got the horses plunging through already deep puddles toward their shed. Boy, howdy, did they race to get in. Snorting and sorting out exactly where each would stand in the shed took a minute or two. When they had decided on their position, they stood watching the lightning show. Mother Nature puts on the best firework displays in the Texas skies.

Storms are part of life at the ranch and they do pass. May any storm in your world also pass.

TTFN,
Mia

Narcissus at the Water Bowl

Howdy, all:

Phoenix, the gray cat, has been a fixture at the ranch since she *arose* from the asphalt about nine years ago. She has her very own habits and ways of doing things. Some of these are based on the fact that she is visually impaired.

She manages to get herself fed and fed quite well. Some would say she is plump. Others would say that she has filled out quite nicely and will survive any famine in the future. With her plumpness comes, well again, some would say, a certain lack of activity. She regards this as her energy-saving plan. With her plan comes one downside. Sometimes she suffers from a condition politely called slow colonic transit time—constipation in other parlance.

To combat this condition, she is encouraged to drink water. She has her very own bowl, set near her food plate. Convenience is her calling card. Phoenix has taken to this plan with all the vigor she can muster. She lets herself down in a feline sprawl by the water bowl. And Narcissus-like, she dunks her face into the water bowl and drinks and drinks. She likes to do this for what seems an interminable amount of time. But it has had its desired effect: no more slow colonic events have occurred. Yeah.

Some things occur slowly but steadily here at the ranch. May your progress always be measured.

TTFN,
Mia

Friends, Large and Small

Howdy, all:

A wonderful scene took place the other day here at the ranch. It went like this.

Prince, Carry, and Wiggles were all happily munching away on the north slope by the house. Wiggles, being Wiggles, was off more or less by herself. Prince and Carry were grazing in tandem, mirroring each other as they slowly made their way across the slope.

Arnold the Armadillo came onto the scene. He was also busy doing what armadillos do— waddling in the armed car shell across the slope. Prince and Carry saw him. They were curious but not frightened. They continued their munching, and, as if choreographed, Prince took to Arnold's right side and Carry to his left. The three of them slowly meandered and munched. Wiggles remained to the side and let the other two escort Arnold across the slope. A very peaceful scene.

Friends large and small are here at the ranch. May you have friends of all sorts in your world.

TTFN,
Mia

Getting Ready for the Holidays

Howdy, all:

Preparations for the holidays always include cleaning—the house, the yard, the feed shed, and of course the ranch truck.

Now this ranch truck has traveled a few miles and sustained a few bumps and bruises from ranch life. It is, though, a very useful conveyance. It should get a *spiffing-up* every now and then and why not at Christmas. Prince and Carry think so.

The other day, while Wiggles was at the hitching post, Prince and Carry got to work cleaning the truck. They had just been given treats. After they get treats, they will "wash a truck" or any vehicle that is close by. They just start a *lickin'* away! Carry started at the front end of the truck; Prince tackled the back. Prince even cleaned up the bed of the truck of the leftover alfalfa stems. Whatta guy!

The truck looks so good right now. It is ready for Santa and Christmas. So if your vehicles need a wash, all it will cost ya are some horse treats. Just dial 1-800-HORSEWASH.

Spiffed up for the Holidays here at the ranch. May your Christmastime be filled with joy.

TTFN,
Mia

Melancholia at the Ranch

Howdy, all:

There is a mood of melancholy on the ranch. Recently, things have been a bit out of sorts here in Central Texas. It appears the critters have picked up on this mood.

The deer have been sporadic in their visits to the backyard feed line. Likewise, the big group of turkeys, complete with the two whitish gray-colored turkeys, have been infrequent in their visits. And finally, the noisy whistling ducks have not been around for some time. Their nonstop chatter is missed.

At least the horses and cows have been more or less regular in their habits. Their presence is always a comfort even in melancholic times. In fact, Jet, the black calf, has made his forays into the yard through the nonelectric fence, and chasing him has been a source of regular exercise.

The mood at the ranch is always better with a good chase. May your chase be a source of contentment.

TTFN,
Mia

A Wonderful Start to the New Year

Howdy, all:

There are celebrations when a New Year's babe arrives. Likewise, here on the ranch, there is rejoicing with a new life. Here is what happened.

Beauty had a cute, cute calf born the other day. It has the longest legs ever and is a chocolate-brown color. "Prima" has made her entrance into the bovine world.

Now, Beauty wanted to make sure that all were aware of her newborn. She came out and had Prima with her and stood right smack dab in the middle of the road where all could see. Prima was busy feeding, so she was occupied. But Beauty stood smartly with head up gazing at all the other cows, making sure they noticed her New Year's calf.

To celebrate further, some coastal hay found its way right at Beauty's feet. She deigned to munch while Prima suckled. The other cows were served some coastal to join in the party. Yum, fresh coastal hay to start the New Year.

Here's to the New Year at the ranch. May your New Year bring much joy and happiness.

TTFN,
Mia

Two for the New Year

Howdy, all:

Well, the story of Beauty and her new calf, Prima, is not the end of the joy for the New Year. Gigi, the beautiful white Brahma cow, has had her calf.

The other day, Gigi was staying off by herself down by the creek. She kept searching for the perfect spot to have her calf. Where she ended up having it remains a secret. She really hid herself well—even though she is white as the day is long.

Here is the funny thing though. Gigi is white. Big Daddy Shirley is white, and the calf is jet-black.

Hmm. Maybe there was an interloper somewhere? Oh, speaking of Shirley. Shirley got picked up by the cowboy sheriff because he had jumped the fence a number of times and ended up on the highway. Shirley will hopefully make his return soon if he pays his bail out of bovine *jail*. Donations can be sent to 1-800-FreeShirley.

Back to Gigi and her newborn calf. The calf's name is "Chip," a chip off the ol' block so to speak.

The New Year is already full of surprises here at the ranch. May your world have surprises too.

TTFN,
Mia

My Very Own Way

Howdy, all:

It has been interesting to observe the different *cow-sonalities* that each bovine has. Over the years, some of the cows have been named for their quirks of habit.

One cow that stands out is Pig Pen. There simply has not been a cow that goes her own way, follows her own cowbell, like Pig Pen. And the latest example of her blazing her own trail was observed the other day. It goes as follows.

Okay, in the Big Sandy Pasture, there is a gate that is used by the LCRA (Lower Colorado River Authority). On the other side of the gate is the neighbor's pasture. That pasture happens to be vacant of critters at this time.

Pig Pen wanted to graze on the greener grass on the other side of the gate. So she got down on her front knees, got her head under the gate, and grazed. Her behind was tilted to the heavens while she feasted on the greener grass under the gate. It sure tasted good. After a good while, Pig Pen got back up and had the most satisfied cow smile on her face. "Yum, yum," she mooed.

Some critters here at the ranch are undaunted by obstacles. May you be so bold in your world.

TTFN,
Mia

Wood Duck Haven

Howdy, all:

The creek area is such a blessing to the ranch. So much of the wildlife depends on the water and woods that the creek offers.

The bridge crossing the creek is now serving as a haven for a pair of wood ducks. These two are hanging out by the bridge because at regular daily intervals, a handful of corn or two appears on the creek banks. Mr. and Mrs. Woody Duck gobble up the corn and then fly down the creek to their secret lair. The hope is for a few more wood ducks to appear.

Now other critters move about the creek. The deer and turkeys and a few raccoons for good measure have been hanging out by the creek. In the winter months, water is not so scarce as in the heat of a Texas summer. But the forest that surrounds the creek provides good cover for all to hide and hunt and nest with their young.

The ranch is blessed with the creek area. May your world have its very own special area.

TTFN,
Mia

Comings and Goings

Howdy, all:

Recently here at the ranch, there have been some comings and goings. And they go like this.

One of the main characters back at the ranch is Shirley, the white-colored bull. He was last seen heading off to cow jail because he had gotten out and was on the road. So someone or by some power, he has gotten out of jail and is back with his gals.

Fleabite and Tweedle-Dum have left the ranch. Hopefully, they will be back soon. Cream Puff, Tweedle-Dum's calf, bellowed mightily after she left. Parting of mom and calf is a bittersweet event, always. Speaking of bellowing, the mornings are often punctuated with the cows mooing. It can be as beautiful as anything Mozart composed.

The black-bellied whistling ducks have returned. They had been absent for a while. But true to form, they have returned to gaggle about the feeding area in the backyard.

And the turkeys and deer are now more regular visitors to the feedline. Their comings and goings always provide some entertainment.

Here at the ranch, critters come and go. May your travels be filled with adventures in your world.

TTFN,
Mia

A Surprise Arrives

Howdy, all:

At this time, surprises of the good kind are most welcome, are they not? Here at the ranch, that is so true.

So Chip and Primo, the two li'l calves of Gigi and Beauty, are growing like weeds. They play so well together; one would think they were siblings (friendly siblings, that is)! Into their world has come a third playmate.

It happened this way. Pig Pen had been missing for a day or two. The thought was that maybe she had pulled her usual escape artist routine. Wiggles was about to be saddled to go look for her. Just like a movie script, at that very moment, out of the woods, came Pig Pen with her new li'l one in tow. She proudly joined the herd down by the Big Muddy. The little calf stayed so very close to her; one would have thought it was attached by wires!

So a fitting name for this calf is Surprise.

The ranch has had a good surprise. May your world yield likewise.

TTFN,
Mia

Clash of the Titans

Howdy, all:

As you may be aware, Shirley, the runaway bull, has come back to the ranch. Along with him has come a coterie of cows with their calves in tow. Cows such as Fleabite, Spot, Tigger, BNW, Gigi's sister, and others have returned. The total number of cows on the ranch is twenty-four.

Ah, but also, too came a twenty-fifth cow—Beef Master, a very big Hereford bull. Oh, boy, the fun started when he showed up. Beef Master and Shirley, just like sumo wrestlers, locked heads, and had a number of shoving matches. These behemoths shoved and pushed their hooves, making grooves in the soft soil. At times, they would stand facing each other, a *huffin'* and a *puffin'*. And then the shoving match would start again.

This clash between these two big, and they are big, bulls went on for a day or two. Now, there is peace at the ranch as each bull has its own *herd*. What is so funny is that the calves were having their very own shoving matches while they cavort and run about. Their little skirmishes are small clashes compared to the clash of the titans!

Tranquility reigns here at the ranch. May there be tranquility in your world too.

TTFN,
Mia

Special Edition—the Mystery Miracle

Howdy, all:

Today is Wiggles's eleventh birthday. She was a miracle horse, or perhaps some would say a mystery horse.

Eleven years ago, just after a morning thunderstorm came to a close (this really did happen), Prince came running up to the hitching post by the garage, snorting and pawing to announce the arrival of Wiggles. Carry, her momma, had just given birth to her under a tree just yonder a bit from the garage. Who Wiggles's daddy is is still a mystery to this day.

You see, Carry was a rescue horse buy. She was nothing but a "hank of hair and a bag of bones" when first purchased. All that has changed—for sure. But no mention by the seller that she was pregnant. And no thought that such a skinny horse could be pregnant. (The seller is out of business, so there is no way of tracking down how Carry got pregnant.)

The little mystery horse has added so much to the life here at the ranch. But today, her first gray hair was found in her forelock. Oh, my, time for some Clairol!

A mystery miracle is being celebrated here at the ranch. May your day be marked with such an event.

TTFN,
Mia

More Food, Foo'

Howdy, all:

Mr. Tom-Tom Turkey (he is Tom-Tom because he is really big) is a regular visitor to the feed line in the backyard. He struts in in the morning and has a good breakfast. Then, he ventures down the slope, checking on his harem. The females are busy with their nests, hopefully bringing forth a batch of turkets.

Some days, he shows up with one or two of the female turkeys, and he proudly guards them while they eat. He puffs up his feathers, and his snood becomes especially red as he faces any and all intruders. The females eat their fill and then disappear into the brush to their hidden nests.

Later in the morning, he goes to the north side of the house and, in true turkey fashion, starts gobble-gobbling his morning cry to all. Today, he added a twist to his message. He turned toward the house and sent a clear signal—"More food, foo'!"

After having delivered his order, he puffed up his feathers even more and strutted back to the food line. More food is forthcoming, sir!

Orders are followed here at the ranch. May your world be orderly too.

TTFN,
Mia

MIA or, really, CIA

Howdy, all:

The other day, it was noted that Gigi, the white Brahma cow, was missing—MIA or cow in absentia. Her sister and all the other cows were accounted, and her calf was in the herd also. Hmm.

Gigi is such an attentive momma that she would not simply wander off and leave her growing calf. A heavy rainfall received the other day caused some minor flooding. The concern was that maybe she got caught and had washed downstream. But no sign of that happening. Buzzards circling is a sign of where something might be down. No buzzards were circling.

No fences were down, and no reports from neighbors of a wandering cow. Where was the ol' gal?

Well, last evening, down by the Big Muddy, Gigi reappeared but looked so very skinny. Her cowboy owner was alerted. Maybe she had another calf? Hopefully, time will tell a good tale.

Life is a circle here at the ranch. May your world's circle be unbroken.

TTFN,
Mia

The Bovine Beatitudes in Honor of Gigi

Howdy, all:

Life is sometimes hard on the ranch. This past week, Gigi disappeared again. This time, she was down and not coming back. Today, she went to Cow Heaven. It is a beautiful sunny day: perfect for her journey. In her honor, and for all cows, here is the "Bovine Beatitudes."

Blessed are the shy, for theirs are the hidden pastures.

Blessed are those who mourn the loss of their calf, for they will be comforted with another calf.

Blessed are the timid, for they will inherit the pasture.

Blessed are those who hunger and thirst, for they will be filled.

Blessed are the momma cows, for they will multiply the herd.

Blessed are those with pure milk, for they will see their calves grow strong.

Blessed are those who suffer silently, for theirs is the Kingdom of Green Pastures.

Blessed are Gigi and all the cows when all kinds of evil are done against them. Blue skies and green pastures await them.

Her calf is doing well. She is strong and beautiful and has taken to the herd like a champ.

Life goes on here at the ranch without the ol' gal. May your sorrows be lifted by blue skies.

TTFN,
Mia

The Love Affair

Howdy, all:

While the Orwellian miasma in the world swirls, life here at the ranch swirls around the latest love affair. It is as follows.

Wiggles is in love with one of the neighbor's horses, Svengali. Oh, boy, does she love to nicker and whinny and stretch her neck over the fence to nuzzle with Svengali. She and Carry and Prince go every weekend to the far end of the pasture to visit the neighbor's horses, and Wiggles visits her beau.

The other day, she and Svengali were planning their honeymoon, or rather their carrot moon. It was evening feeding time. Wiggles gave Svengali one last horse smooch and dashed to her feed bucket. Poor Svengali was beside himself. He raced up and down the fence line, whinnying and carrying on. "Oh, where have you gone, my sweet equine pet! Come back, come back!" he cried. Wiggles ate faster than usual and threw her bucket high in the air and raced back to Svengali. They then continued their horse smooching and making plans. Their invitations will come by Pony Express.

Carrots and love are all the rage here at the ranch. May your world be filled with such sweets.

TTFN,
Mia

Curious Georgina

Howdy, all:

Pig Pen is back and has another calf. That calf has earned the name Curious Georgina. This is how she has earned her name.

She is one of the cutest li'l rascals around. She loves to sneak into the horse pasture. What she does is get her nose under the lowest strand of smooth wire and then does the cow limbo under the fence. She is quite proficient at this maneuver. Then, true to her name, she checks everything out in the pasture. The horses simply ignore her nosing around.

This morning, Curious Georgina got out of the horse pasture and came over to the hitching post. Wiggles was being saddled for a morning ride. She thought she should come along too. Maybe a saddle for Georgina?

She also comes over to the golf cart and sticks her head in looking for anything good to eat. If she finds nothing, she then licks the windshield on the cart giving it a good cow wash.

For the young ones here at the ranch, there is much to be curious about. May your world spark some curiosity.

TTFN,
Mia

A Cool Place to Live

Howdy, all:

With summer bringing the heat from Hades to Texas, the critters seek cool shelter with a couple of qualities. Shade and access to any breeze are at the top of the list of qualities as is access to water.

That is why Mr. and Mrs. Toad have moved into the Well House. It is a cool building with a window that catches the breezes. Most importantly, it has a steady supply of water. The toads enjoy the regular feast of the little bugs that are found in the Well House. Hopefully, there are more toads on their way to augment that population in Toad Hall. Hind legs crossed!

Dorothy the Deer has a new fawn. She and the fawn are escaping the heat by staying down by the creek. The woods offer some very nice shade and handfuls of corn can also be found there—by some quirk of magic!

Staying cool at the ranch is important. May you keep your cool in your world.

TTFN,
Mia

Love Takes a Hiatus for the Summer

Howdy, all:

So Wiggles and Svengali are having to spend some time apart this summer. It goes like this.

In the summer months, the beans, or seeds, of the mesquite trees come out in full bloom. They are plump and juicy. Very enticing treats to munch on for the horses and cows. And especially so since the green grass of spring has long faded to brown under the hot summer sun of Texas.

And there is always one in the crowd; it is Carry. A few years ago, she ate one too many of the mesquite beans, causing her to seriously founder or go lame. Now, she must be kept from eating those beans.

During the months of July through to early September, Carry is kept quarantined (don't we love that word?) from the mesquite. Thus, the horses are kept in a small pasture that is free of all mesquite. That means Wiggles is separated from Svengali during this time. Ah, love must take a break. Darn.

Fear not, this time shall pass, and love will bloom again. In your world, may separation make the love stronger.

TTFN,
Mia

BNW Joins the Momma Crowd

Howdy, all:

There is a black-and-white cow, BNW. She has been a lonely cow, always off by herself and so very quiet in her demeanor. She would often be the last cow coming up the hill in the evenings.

The other day, BNW had a calf. Oh, gosh, the calf is a spitting image of her—an absolute copy—the white face, black body, and half-white legs. This calf is at her side, and BNW is so very proud.

A few weeks ago, BBC, the big black cow, had had her calf. The calf was a smoky gray; thus, Smokey is his name. Smokey is now so very happy to have a playmate. These two calves now engage daily in calf games while their respective mommas graze the day away.

No more alone here at the ranch. May you have companionship in your world too.

TTFN,
Mia

A Few Developments

Howdy, all:

The "fires of hell" have come to Texas in the form of oppressive heat. So make straight your ways, oh, Texas folks and critters!

In the midst of the heat, some developments have occurred. Smokey, the new calf of BBC, has changed colors. He has gone from smoky gray to a smoky tan color. So his name has changed to Buttercup (in honor of some folks *ranging* through swamps and mountains with a bunch of gear on).

And Buttercup and Pirate, BNW's calf, have found their way into the yard where they checked out the feed line and the birdbath watering dish.

Tucked in a corner of the mesquite patch marking the spot where Wiggles was born is a cute figure on a tree. It is under this tree that Wiggles was born. This marker is almost as cute as Wiggles!

In spite of the heat, things keep a *happenin'* here at the ranch. May you keep moving too.

TTFN
Mia

Watch Where You Put Your Nose

Howdy, all:

There is a silly horse that resides on the ranch—loveable but silly. And that horse is Wiggles. Here is what happened to that delightfully entertaining horse the other day.

Wiggles put her nose where it did not belong—she either nuzzled a wasp nest or a nonvenomous snake. Her snout became quite swollen. She was standing looking quite forlorn in the pasture, which is so atypical of her. The vet suggested some anti-inflammatory and pain medications for her. Wiggles started eating after a couple of hours, which is always a good sign. Hopefully, she has learned to keep her snout where it does not belong.

On an aside, the black-bellied whistling ducks have shown back up with their young ones. Ah, the noisy clamor has returned to the backyard.

All is well and noisy here at the ranch. May you keep your nose clean in your world too.

TTFN
Mia

The Pecking Order

Howdy, all:

Among the animals on the ranch, there is a pecking order. It goes like this.

At the top of the order are the horses. If Carry wants a particular blade of grass, the cows will move from that area. Funny to see a huge cow give way to a horse even though the horse is fairly large.

Next comes the cows, even a calf. For example, No Tail, a young calf with no tail, did not like the turkeys in his area of the pasture. He chased both the hens and the big toms out of *his* pasture. The turkeys darted through the fence, and the big toms flew over the fence.

The next rung is occupied by the turkeys. The big toms were in the backyard having their breakfast when a number of deer tried to horn in on the food. Well, the tom turkeys, with their long, goose-like necks, chased the deer away from the food. (Willa Cather likened geese to "hissing snakes on stilts." We could include turkeys in that characterization.)

The deer are next in order, for they move the whistling ducks when they wish to feed. And, finally, the ducks scare the doves away. Poor doves and small songbirds must wait for all the others to move before they get their chance at the food in the backyard. Hmm.

That is the order of life on the ranch. May your world have some order in it.

TTFN,
Mia

The Garage Is My Bedroom

Howdy, all:

There are two cats on the ranch. One is orange-and-white, that is, Mr. Peekaboo. Peekaboo chases deer and grasshoppers and leaves his paw prints on the windows of the truck.

The other cat, ah, the other cat is Phoenix. She takes napping to an art form. She is what some would call Texas plump, fluffy, well-filled out, and other descriptive terms. She has taken over the garage as her boudoir for the night. She stretches out in all her grayness right by the step into the garage. And there she snoozes all night long.

It seems as if that cat realizes that being close to her litter box is well worth making the garage her bedroom. Just a few steps to take care of business. Not a bad plan.

So here is to convenience at the ranch. May you have some conveniences in your world.

TTFN,
Mia

Well, Why Can't I?

Howdy, all:

There is a full moon, and it is Halloween. Unusual things are bound to happen even here at the ranch. And although it is not that unusual, Pig Pen is involved.

Pig Pen is one of the ranch's favorites. She is a blondish color, actually a dirty-blond color, and her coat is always in disarray. Her ears are a bit too large for her face, but they seem to make her even more endearing. By the way, those ears can hear the rustle of a feedbag miles away.

The horse pasture has a smooth wire fence around it versus barbed wire. You know, those spoiled horses can't possibly get a nick or cut from barbwire: heavens, no! Pig Pen has figured this out. She has also figured out how to squeeze between the smooth wires and get into the horse pasture whenever she wants. She will come trotting up the hill all by her lonesome and "let herself in" the horse pasture.

Her break-in move was noted, and some ties were added to the smooth wires so that they could not be pushed apart. Pig Pen came up to the fence, attempted her break-in, and was stymied. With her distinct face and those big ears, she turned and gave a look that said: "Well, why can't I go in?"

Many residents here at the ranch are very endearing even in their antics. May your world be so filled.

TTFN,
Mia

It's Turkey Time

Howdy, all:

Thanksgiving is coming up soon. And guess which critter has made their appearance en masse? Yup, the turkey gang.

There are twenty-two turkeys in this one gang. Two of them are big tom turkeys; the others are quite a bit smaller and appear to be young. Yesterday morning, they were feasting in the backyard at the food. The young females hop and flap their wings. The two tom turkeys strut and puff up their feathers. So what we have is not the Harlem Globetrotters but the Turkey Hoppers and Strutters.

There are two other tom turkeys that have been banished from this group. They hang around just outside the imaginary territorial line of the big gang. When no one is looking, they sneak in for a gobble or two.

We have turkey here at the ranch. May you have a table full of thanks.

TTFN,
Mia

Cleanup on Aisle Three

Howdy, all:

Mother Nature is really quite amazing. She has her own cleanup crew. That crew in Texas consists of big black birds also known as buzzards. These buzzards are indeed Texas-sized.

In flight, they are very graceful. They soar and glide with their wings spread wide and make flight look effortless. When not flying, the buzzards sit in the tops of trees or on one of their favorite perches, the tower for the power line. One of the funny things to see is how they "dry their wings out." They perch on the rungs of the power line tower and stretch out their massive wings. And they sit with those wings outstretched for a long time. Quite a sight to see.

Up close, these birds are quite ugly. Good thing there are no Mother Nature mirrors! But they do a good job of keeping the *aisles* clean, and one can always tell where the latest *spill* is by watching where they are circling.

The job of cleaning up is important here at the ranch. Here's hoping your world is kept tidy too.

TTFN,
Mia

I Was Here

Howdy, all:

One of the simplest pleasures of ranch life is handing out treats to the horses. Oh, the joy of giving! And the horses are so very grateful for the sweet treats.

These three expert beggars line up just outside the fake electric fence by the garage door. Anytime that garage door is open, there is a possibility for a treat. Prince, Carry, and Wiggles have that Pavlovian instinct regarding the garage door!

Once the treats are given, they smack their lips with contented looks on their faces. Prince gives both Carry and Wiggles *kisses*, and then Carry and Prince go over to the vehicles. They give *smooches* to the car and truck, leaving their mark—a scratch or two on the vehicle hoods. When you see these love marks, you will know, "I was here." (Wiggles just keeps smacking her lips.)

Treats give contentment here at the ranch. May you have a treat or two in your world.

TTFN,
Mia

The New Year with New Cows

Howdy, all:

What a heckuva year. The cows want to ring in the New Year in fashion. So added to the herd are two sister cows. They both have horns, which make them look a bit intimidating, but both are really quite skittish. Hazella and Myrtle are their names.

Hazella is a beautiful brown cow with a sheen of hazel caramel in her coat. Myrtle is darker brown. And just like sisters from a Jane Austen novel, they travel together and seem to enjoy each other's company.

The rest of the herd have accepted these new cows quite well. Good ol' Shirley, the bull, does his part and makes sure they feel part of the group.

A new year dawns here at the ranch. The last day of the year brought significant rain. Perhaps that portends for some green spring grass.

A new year, new cows, good news here at the ranch. May your new year have good news too.

TTFN,
Mia

The Pensive Pony

Howdy, all:

There can be few horses in the world that have more personality than Wiggles. Some of her qualities make her endearing: other qualities can make her, well, let's just say, make her Wiggles.

One of her qualities is acting as the *pensive pony* when she is ridden. When starting out a ride and going away from Prince and Carry, she finds a lot to look at and ponder. "Oh, look, there is a leaf stirring in the breeze. Let me stop and stare at it for a long, long time," says the pensive pony. "And over there, a bird in a tree. My gosh, haven't seen one of those for at least two seconds!"

These elongated staring moments only occur on the ride out. There are no pensive moments on the return trip. Oh, no, my gosh no! "What leaf, what bird?" says the pony. "Time to get home, get this saddle off, roll and eat carrots, and play with Prince and Carry."

The ride home here at the ranch is a fast one. May the return to your home be swift.

TTFN,
Mia

The Big Flock

Howdy, all:

In these winter months, the ducks can be a bit flighty, no pun intended, in their attendance to the backyard feeding line. Sometimes they show up just in the morning; sometimes, just in the evening. And sometimes, they don't show up at all.

Recently, however, they have been showing up in big numbers. Boy, howdy, there are a lot of them. This morning, the entire convention of ducks was present! They do carry on so; their chatter is incessant.

These ducks are no quacking fools. They have figured out that if they *clean up* the feeding line, there is a chance that more food will be put out. So they eat their fill, fly down to the Big Muddy, and then come back for an appetizer or two.

Some of the ducks will sit on top of the house—just like ducks in a shooting gallery. They sit up there until they see more food put out. Then, they will glide down and start announcing to the others at the Big Muddy. "Come and get it!"

Noisy and crowded here at the ranch these days. Hope your world is lively too.

TTFN,
Mia

Ice and Snow Cometh

Howdy, all:

Central Texas is not known for big snowstorms, storms that bring inches of snow that stay for days and days. If anything, the sight of a single snowflake causes everyone to grab their cameras and dash out to take a picture of it. Well, there are now a lot of flakes here at the ranch, usually the land of snakes, scorpions, cactus, et al.

The critters on the ranch are weathering this unusual patch fairly well. Prince, Carry, and Wiggles have checked in to Stable Inn. This inn serves meals twice a day with snacks provided when the sun peaks out and water is served chilled.

Wiggles has taken up a new sport. It is called snow removal. She clears areas where she thinks there may be a tender morsel. She paws the snow away to get at that treat. She does a good job wherever she *puts a hoof to.*

So as with Texas heat, the critters figure things out. May all in your world do likewise.

TTFN,
Mia

The Aftermath of the Ice Storm

Howdy, all:

Overall, things are back to normal here at the ranch after the ice storm from hell. Hell had frozen over!

The horses are happy. The melting snow has made for beautiful sprigs of fresh green grass. They have turned their noses up at coastal hay.

The cows have been shuffled about. Pig Pen made her last escape, and so now is at another ranch. Darn. Pirate and Buttercup, two of the older calves, have been separated from their mommas, and they also have been moved. Their mommas, BNW and BBC, have been wailing and gnashing their cud for the past day. Thank goodness their memories are limited.

The new calves, Romulus and Remus, have the run of the ranch. Blue Tag may be giving birth to a calf soon. This cow has a blue tag on one of her ears.

The wood ducks continue to enjoy the corn fed to them at the creek's edge.

The ice is gone, and life continues here at the ranch. May life in your world continue too.

TTFN,
Mia

The Three Magi Visit

Howdy, all:

From time to time, the ranch has unusual visitors. This last week was such a time.

Part of the story involves the curse of Texas, the wild hogs that populate Texas. They are such a nuisance. They can be hunted and trapped, but they are so prolific that they are always present. Over the years, the ranch has had its share of wild hogs. Every now and then, some lead poisoning is administered, and they go away for a while. Well, this past month, after the ice storm, the hogs found their way back to the ranch. They were *'helping out* by tilling up the Big Sandy pasture. Hmm.

The hunt was on to get those *tillin'* hogs. But they are very, very wily and of course no sign of them during the hunt. Well, onto the scene came the Three Magi. Out of nowhere, three healthy big dogs showed up. Friendly dogs but big and strong. Where and to whom do these dogs belong to? No one claimed them. But the next day, the dogs were seen chasing the hogs up the creek and off into the wilderness.

Since that day, no hogs, no dogs, no more tilled pastures. The Magi did the trick.

The ranch appreciates any help it can get. Here's hoping you get the help you need.

TTFN,
Mia

The Hunt Is On

Howdy, all:

So the Magi did not quite get rid of the wild hogs. One of the Magi, Caspar, has found himself a better home than wandering the mesquite prairie of the ranch. So perhaps Melchior and Balthazar will also find their way to a good home.

All that remains is for the hogs to either change their locale or to have their locale changed for them. Rumors are that there is hog heaven.

Texas likes to brag about being home to the biggest whatever, and Mr. Gargantuan, the leader of the hog gang, is Texas big. One would also have to say that he is ugly. Although I don't think Texas wants to brag about their big and ugly things! Hahaha!

Mr. G. hangs out by the creek. He is being sought by many. Maybe, just maybe, during the week of a full moon, he will be found and sent to hog heaven. So if you are in the neighborhood, you may hear a bang and another bang. Just know that noise is for a good cause.

Here's hoping the balance is restored here at the ranch. May your world be balanced.

TTFN,
Mia

Watch Horses

Howdy, all:

Did you know that horses make great *watchdogs*? That is, they are akin to having very large dogs. However, they do not bark. But, boy, do they let you know that something or someone is approaching.

Wiggles, Prince, and Carry are very good at detecting when something is amiss. Wiggles seems to be especially keen on things out of the ordinary. The other day, she led the charge to the far end of the coastal pasture when some of the neighbor's cows showed up unexpectedly. She snorted and raced toward them with her tail a *flyin'* and head held high and eyes trained on the spot where the cows poked their heads from the mesquite brush.

With the hunt for the hogs, the horses are very good at finding where they hide. Wiggles was saddled up, and sure enough, she found them. The hogs were on the little isthmus formed by the dry creek and the running creek. So hopefully now the hunt can be a bit more successful.

The ranch has its own equine guard brigade. May your world have such delightful guards.

TTFN,
Mia

121

Momma Gets to Eat

Howdy, all:

Now that some of the wild hogs have found their way to hog heaven, the deer and turkeys are returning to the ranch, specifically the feed line in the backyard.

The younger deer crouch down and squeeze under the mostly fake electric fence surrounding the yard. The grown deer do a little leap over it.

Just this morning, the deer family came to feed. Momma Deer, Dorothy, had three young deer with her. They all started to munch away. Dorothy patrolled the area to make sure there were no dangers, such as the orange-and-white panther. She then started to eat. One of the young deer tried to nibble a treat near her. With her hooves, she admonished him, giving the very distinct message: "Momma gets to eat, and without interruption, thank you very much."

Respect for our parents is enforced here at the ranch. Perhaps likewise in your world too?

TTFN,
Mia

Two Ducks, Two Deer, and One Cat

Howdy, all:

The other morning, there were two ducks and two deer feeding in the backyard. The two ducks are a faithful couple that shows up most days. The two deer are young female deer that have just found the feeding area.

These critters were enjoying the morning feast when upon this idyllic scene came a very dangerous cat, probably a panther disguised as an orange-and-white housecat. Slowly, slowly, slowly crept this creature of prey upon the unsuspecting deer. Forget the ducks, the cat was going for a big game!

The hunt was on. The cat, scrunching itself low to the ground, crawled cautiously toward the deer. Finally, he was in striking distance. The moment had arrived. This housecat was going to bring down a big deer and have it for breakfast, ladies and gents. He dashed at the deer like a bolt of lightning. *Boing, boing, boing,* the deer jumped and cleared the fake electric fence, well out of range of the feline.

Hmm. No deer for breakfast. The cat turns and slowly saunters back to his lair. Meanwhile, the ducks are watching all of this wondering: *What the heck! We thought cats hunted birds?*

Perseverance may pay off here at the ranch one day. May you stick with it until you succeed.

TTFN,
Mia

The Blossoming after the Storm

Howdy, all:

The ranch was hit by a biblical-like storm the other evening. One would have thought the temple curtains were torn again! Wind, rain, lightning came crashing in from the north. It was blowing so hard that the rain was falling sideways, and that is not a Texas tale.

After the storm, just as in the books and stories of old, the next morning dawned bright and sunny. The critters emerged to see what the heck had happened.

Mr. Tom Turkey was in the backyard, doing a turkey trot dance, which consists of hopping about, turning around 180 degrees, and shaking his tail feathers. The deer came in and gobbled up all they could eat, jostling one another for the best morsel. And the ducks kept up a cacophony among all these critters.

A wonderful event happened the night before the storm. A new calf was born. Stormy was born to one of the BBCs. (There are about four big black cows on the ranch.)

Another creature who came out to survey the poststorm landscape was Twiggy, the local bobcat. She was sunning herself in the coastal pasture, wondering what all the clatter of the last evening was about.

"A dark and stormy night," wrote Snoopy. And that is what it was here at the ranch. May your storms pass in your world.

TTFN,
Mia

The Parade, Ranch Style

Howdy, all:

Summer is the time for parades. Fourth of July is just around the corner, and many locales will have their own red, white, and blue celebrations. The ranch will not be outdone when it comes to celebrations.

The ranch-style parades happen in the evening when some of the Texas heat has dissipated. (*Some* is a relative term.) The parade consists primarily of cows. The other critters, the deer, rabbits, and so forth are sometimes inadvertent participants. The horses may also join in. They march for carrots!

There are now eight calves on the ranch, and they provide the entertainment in the parade. Each one has its very own show as the cows march up the hill to the cool water trough by the feed shed. For example, Vanilla Bean loves to rear up, paw the air with her hooves, and then leap and jump about with her tail high in the air. She gins up Stormy and Freckles to join her in these antics. Pieface darts about chasing these younger calves, and Romulus, Remus, and Bandito contribute by racing in and around the momma cows as they march.

Grab an ice tea and join the ranch celebrations. May you have a joyous gathering in your world.

TTFN,
Mia

The Turkey Triumvirate

Howdy, all:

New additions to the ranch are always so looked forward to; new calves, fawns, ducks, and more come into the circle of life. And each creature has its own special way of introducing the next generation to ranch life.

Momma T (Turkey) brings her chicks out very cautiously. One can imagine the number of predatory critters that would love turkey dinner. This year, Momma T has three chicks. To see them is a real treat. They are elusive and very fast to find cover.

These three chicks are lively. When seen, they are happily following Momma T. They seem to be on a leash, of sorts, only straying a short distance from her. When they need to catch up, they flap their wings and dash about the ground in a madcap fashion, nearly colliding with her plump behind.

Yesterday, she brought them to the backyard. They set about scratchin', hoppin', and peckin' in delight. But as soon as Momma T noticed a strange sight, off into the woods the triumvirate scampered following their mom.

A pleasant sight to see new life here at the ranch. May your world have the same pleasantness.

TTFN,
Mia

The Moo Doesn't Fall Far from the Cow

Howdy, all:

One of the ranch's most endearing cows is Pig Pen. She is an adorable escape artist. She is homely, but she is also one of the most prolific cows in the bunch. She earns her keep by producing some of the cutest and rascally calves imaginable.

Her latest calf is no exception. Petunia is a chip off the old block. Petunia gets herself into all the places she is not supposed to be. For example, she has learned to squeeze under the smooth wire fence to get into the horse pasture. Wonder where she learned that? Hmm. And then she has learned that the electric fence around the yard is mostly not electric.

She is quite smart. When she realizes she has been caught trespassing, she skedaddles out and races to hide behind Pig Pen. Li'l scamp.

The ranch is home to scamps and saints alike. Probably much like your world.

TTFN,
Mia

What Are You?

Howdy, all:

The other morning, one of the fawns of Dorothy the Deer was playing by Frog Pond. His twin was also there but was occupied munching on some cool, delicious green grass.

This particular fawn was near the gravel road and was more interested in Mr. Beep-Beep, the roadrunner. The roadrunner has made his home near Frog Pond. I am sure it provides him not only cool water but also probably a variety of little snacks that roadrunners like.

The fawn came face-to-face with Mr. Beep-Beep. For his part, Mr. BB stopped and also stared back at the fawn. These two stood stock-still, unusual for both, and continued to eye each other. Running through both of their minds was the question, *And, what are you?*

They did a little dance. The fawn hopped a step or two, the roadrunner trotted a pace or two, and then they stared again at each other. This little duet continued for a few more moments. Finally, each took off at high speed to their respective corners of the world.

Many little wonders here at the ranch. Hopefully in your world, you, too, have some wonders.

TTFN,
Mia

About the Author

Mia Francis grew up in a large rollicking family. Stories abounded and especially stories of the antics of animals were encouraged.

Now, Mia Francis brings some of that storytelling of animals from her ranch to share in this book, *News from the Ranch*.

It is hoped that all will enjoy these true tales, with a dash of spice added, of the animals.

So get a good cup of coffee or a nice cool beverage and enjoy the adventures of the animals of the Texas ranch.

CPSIA information can be obtained
at www.ICGtesting.com
Printed in the USA
BVHW090005210622
640202BV00007B/47